SUCH LOVELY NEIGHBORS

SUCH LOVELY NEIGHBORS

A PSYCHOLOGICAL THRILLER

JACK DANE

CONTENTS

Prologue 1

1. Nikki 3
2. Nikki 10
3. Nikki 20
4. Nikki 25
5. Nikki 31
6. Nikki 36
7. Nikki 42
8. Nikki 47
9. Nikki 53
10. Nikki 60
11. Nikki 67
12. Nikki 75
13. Nikki 81
14. Nikki 87
15. Nikki 97
16. Nikki 103
17. Nikki 110
18. Nikki 115
19. Nikki 120
20. Nikki 126
21. Nikki 137
22. Nikki 143
23. Nikki 154
24. Nikki 158
25. Nikki 164
26. Nikki 173
27. Nikki 178
28. Nikki 184

29. Nikki   188

30. Nikki   194

31. Mary   202

32. Mary   208

33. Mary   212

34. Nikki   218

35. Nikki   220

36. Nikki   224

Epilogue   230

Also by Jack DANE   235
ABOUT THE AUTHOR   237

Welcome to the neighborhood...

First-time homeowners Nikki and Noah Anderson are delighted to find an affordable starter home within commuting distance of NYC.

The neighborhood is absolutely adorable, and everyone is so friendly and welcoming. Between potlucks and white picket fences, it's an idyllic suburban dream.

Or is it?

Because something feels...off. The neighbors smile a little *too* much. There are strange sounds in the night. And then there's the pair of wedding rings they find buried in their backyard...

The suburbs have their share of dark secrets, too. And by the time Nikki and Noah realize it, it might already be **too late**.

PROLOGUE

MARY

I'll never get over the perfect peace of waking up in the suburbs.

The sun shining in through my window, the birds chirping just outside—all of it is picture perfect. Our little slice of heaven, far enough away from the hustle and bustle of New York City that we might as well be in a different world.

As I pull apart the bedroom curtains to let in more of that glorious sunlight, I catch the scent of roasted coffee beans. A smile touches my lips. I'll never get over that smell, either.

Ron is downstairs, getting the coffee ready before he has to head off to work.

Distantly, I can make out the sound of a lawnmower running somewhere in the cul-de-sac. I slide the window open, and the warm summer breeze wafts inside.

Ron comes in with two steaming cups of coffee, offering me one along with a smile as he joins me at the window.

Our little slice of heaven. He puts an arm around me as we sip our morning caffeine and look out over the quiet street around us.

What a beautiful day it is. So serene.

As my eyes rove over our meticulously maintained front yard and flowerbeds, I spot our neighbor Joe coming around the side of his house, a big brown leaf bag in hand. The source of the morning lawn mowing noises.

Little bits of grass clippings flutter through the air around him as he hoists the bag up into the back of his truck.

He sets it down and turns, catching sight of Ron and me in the window. Joe gives us a wave, and we wave back. It's wonderful how friendly we all are.

Joe disappears around the side of his house again, and then we hear the mower rev back up.

Ron gives me a squeeze as that summer air washes over us again. I take another sip of the delicious coffee, savoring it for a moment with my eyes closed.

When they open again, I find myself looking at the leaf bag once more.

More specifically, looking at the severed arm sticking out of the top of it.

My heart thuds.

That's right—thank goodness I saw Joe, because I'd nearly forgotten—we get rid of the bodies on Tuesdays.

ONE
NIKKI

Moving might be my least favorite activity in the whole world.

I mean, I think I'd actually prefer getting stuck in an hours-long bar conversation about stocks with a guy who's got halitosis than I would moving ever again.

Then again, this time won't be like our moves in the past. This time, I'm not moving into another tiny NYC apartment on an upper floor with no elevator.

Our first house. Even just thinking about that makes my stomach dance as I finish taping another packed box and glance up at Noah across the room in the kitchen area.

He's talking with one of the movers, double-checking to make sure all our stuff is headed to the right destination.

Realizing I'm looking at him, he winks at me, making me giggle.

"This one's ready," I say, stepping aside to let one of the other moving men pick up the cardboard box.

Not even so much as a grunt. These guys are pros though—I try to breathe easier. I've felt tense all morning, a mix of excitement about the new house coupled with the worry of actually moving in there.

Petey, my teacup poodle, continues yapping heroically at the moving company crew as they tear through his territory. He weighs all of eight pounds, but he has the heart of a two-hundred pound English Mastiff.

I look over at Noah again now that I've finished putting away the living room accessories. He runs a hand through his dirty blonde hair and nods as the mover says something to him. I know it's shallow of me to say, but one of the main reasons I fell for him was that wavy blond hair. And at thirty-nine, his hairline is still holding strong, a good sign.

Appraising the apartment again, I pull a tissue from my pocket and pat the beads of sweat forming along my temples. The place is a hive of activity, men coming in and out as our life in NYC is uprooted for good.

Two of them are working on the couch now, arguing with each other as they maneuver the heavy sectional through the entryway. They're covered in sweat too, and not just from the exertion.

Summer weather is in full swing in the city now that June has arrived. I've got every window in the apartment open to help circulate air—plus plenty of water bottles on ice for everyone—but still, we're all going to be a few pounds lighter by the end of the day.

"Thanks again," Noah says as he steps away from the mover.

He skirts past two men hauling out our floor-standing mirror to make his way over to me.

"All good?" I ask.

Noah nods. "All good. Just wanted to be sure everything we've ever owned didn't end up in Montana or something."

I let out a laugh, which relaxes the tight knot in my stomach a notch. Things are going to be okay. All of this is going to work out perfectly.

Noah notices and pulls me into a hug. I allow my face to press into the fabric of his sleeveless NYU t-shirt and breathe in, his scent filling my nostrils.

I like the smell of him, even a little sweaty. Now that's love.

Petey, never one to miss out on a hug, runs up to us and puts his paws on my leg with a whine. I giggle and scoop him up.

"He told me they should have everything else loaded up within the hour," Noah says as we separate.

Nodding, I feel my stomach pulse once again. The final hour in our apartment.

Ever since we got married earlier this year, we've talked about moving, but it's no longer just talk. This is really, truly happening. I've been in New York City since I was born, so this is a big step.

Noah seems to realize the gravity of it all too as he wraps an arm around my waist and gives me a squeeze.

"End of an era," he says.

The wailing siren of a fire truck from outside interrupts what would've been quite the emotional moment.

Wry smiles break out across both of our faces as we look at each other and try not to laugh.

That's New York for you. Busy, noisy, absolutely chaotic. I love it.

Suburbia will be the polar opposite, and for the longest time, I didn't think I could handle it.

Then I turned thirty-one, and suddenly the one-AM screaming sirens didn't hold that same charm. Neither did having less than a thousand square feet to our names.

Especially not considering the plans we have. Noah looks down at his phone, which has started buzzing with an incoming phone call. He extricates himself from me and steps aside.

"Cable guy," he says before holding up the phone.

That reminds me. I set Petey back down and then press my palms against my pockets, but find no phone. A quick head-dart around the living room doesn't reveal it either. I step into the bedroom, pressing my back up against the wall so a mover can slip past with our bedside lamp.

"Sorry."

"Sorry," we both say at the near collision and smile at each other.

There's my phone, resting on the windowsill. Picking it up, I see I've got two messages from Emma, who wants to wish me goodbye before we officially head out.

Emma's been my best friend since we roomed together freshman year at NYU. As soon as I walked in that first day and saw her hanging up a Led Zeppelin poster, I knew we'd be thick as thieves.

Because she's my best friend, she's also shared in no

uncertain terms how pissed she is that I'm leaving her alone in the city. I tap the screen to open our text message thread and tell her I've finished packing.

Do they have room for me in the moving van? is Emma's response, making me smirk.

She's got a steady boyfriend of her own, Max, but as far as I know, they aren't in a position to buy a home anytime soon.

Honestly, I didn't think we were either, until we stumbled on this place.

Given the state of things, most homes—even starter homes—were a bit of a stretch for us. Then we came across the listing, and it was like everything fell into place.

Another text from Emma comes through. *On my way.*

Fifteen minutes later, I step out of the apartment and take the stairs down to the lobby to meet her.

She's there waiting for me when the doors open, arms spread wide to give me a big hug.

"There's the moving queen," she says, wrapping me up tight.

I squeeze her back, shutting my eyes a moment as we embrace.

"Everything good so far?" she asks.

"Noah's wagon wheel coffee table got scratched, but I've wanted to toss that thing since I first laid eyes on it, so no real loss there," I say.

Emma nods knowingly. "I actually paid the moving guys to rough that thing up. You're welcome, Ki."

I laugh again as we head out of the lobby and into the

sunshine. Instantly I can feel the intense heat of the sun on my skin, and a hot rush of air greets my face.

"Wow," I say. Sweat begins to seep from my pores almost on command.

Emma presses a hand to her eyes as she nods. "You guys picked a hot one, that's for sure."

"Better than pouring rain, I guess."

The big moving van is parked on the street in front of us, the back open and nearly completely full with our belongings. A couple of the movers nod politely to us before wiping their brows and heading back inside.

Emma giggles and pokes me. "One of those guys is actually pretty hot."

I smirk and shake my head. "Nobody tell Max."

She gives me a light slap on the arm. "Oh hush. Max is hot too. In fact, on a day like this, I think everybody in this stinking city is hot."

"Speaking of hot..." Emma adds, making me turn around to face the building again.

Noah is striding out, his hair ruffled by the breeze as he walks toward us and gives Emma a wave. He's got his sunglasses nestled atop his head like a headband.

"Hey stranger," he says.

He and Emma hug then Noah touches my shoulder.

"The guys said they're basically wrapped. Want to head out in about an hour? Is that enough time for you guys?"

"I still can't believe you two are moving," Emma says with a shake of her head.

"Who knows if I'll ever see you guys again...plus, where am I gonna watch the Mets games now?"

"You can come down to visit us and watch," I chuckle. "We're only like an hour train ride away."

Emma shakes her head in disbelief. "A house. A real house. With like, a yard and everything? All to yourselves? No strangers breathing down your neck? No weird sounds coming through the walls?"

Noah nods, a big grin on his face. That was one of the main selling points for him—the quiet. Plus a large yard with a patio to grill out on.

"Big yard. New patio, fire pit, the works."

"I'm so jealous," Emma whines. "You just got married, and now you're getting a *house*. Absolutely kicking my butt at the game of life. How did you two get so lucky?"

Noah shakes his head. "I really don't know. When we first saw the price, we thought it was almost too good to be true."

That was a line my father always used to give me growing up. *If something seems too good to be true, it probably is.*

He'd say it whenever the topic of Mom was brought up.

Well this time, I think we've finally found the exception to the rule.

TWO
NIKKI

Noah glances down at the address on his phone one final time before a big smile spreads across his face.

"Welcome home," he says, his voice rising with excitement.

"Was the neighborhood this cute the last time we were here?" I ask, my heart pounding.

Every house on this tree-lined cul-de-sac is absolutely adorable. Easing the car into the driveway, Noah is all smiles.

My chest flutters as I take in our home. It's two stories with cute white shutters bordering the windows and a light blue siding I fell in love with at first sight. I feel like I'm almost floating on air as I open and shut the passenger side door and get out.

The first thing I notice as I step out of the car is the quiet. It's like a blanket of peace rests over this entire neighborhood.

I let Petey down, warning him not to take off running.

He looks back at me and then shoots across the front yard, running laps with his tongue out.

Noah's door slams shut as he steps out too, stretching his back a moment before striding forward and shaking his head. He throws his arms out to the sides in a *look at this* gesture.

"Are you kidding me?" he asks, the grin growing even wider.

He drops his arms and finds my eyes. "Babe, are you serious? This is actually ours?"

I let out a squeal and run up to him, the two of us hugging and giggling together as he lifts me and does a little spin on the driveway.

When we toured the house, it didn't fully click that we'd actually end up living here. For me, at least.

There was a sense of detachment, like I was viewing some sort of suburban museum rather than scouting out my future living situation.

Now though, it's a different story. It's real. We have keys in hand—all of this is truly ours.

As if on cue, a horn sounds from behind us, and the moving van pulls into the cul-de-sac. The big vehicle lumbers forward, laden down with every bit of furniture we own before finally coming to a squealing stop just beside the driveway.

The moving men pile out of the truck, and then everything gets underway.

The sun continues to beat down overhead as I scurry about, directing the movers and making sure everything arrives in its rightful place without damage.

"Right in here," I say, directing the men bringing the sectional couch into the living room.

There's a nice cream-colored carpet in here, and it already has me stressed out because the movers are leaving bootprints across it.

It would've been kind of strange to ask the movers to remove their shoes every time they came inside, so I didn't say anything, though now I'm slightly regretting it.

The men lower the couch down to the carpet, letting out grunts of exertion. To my left is a wall of windows that looks out over the curved street and the other houses on it. Our front lawn is covered in moving blankets with various pieces of furniture strewn across them, all waiting their turn to be moved inside.

Noah is somewhere upstairs, his muffled voice filtering down from above. We've got Petey up there in his crate for now so he doesn't get stepped on.

"Make sure it's far enough away from the... that's fine," I say, wiping my hand across my brow.

It's got to be like ninety-five degrees out right now, and we're all feeling it. I suck down a water bottle from the pack we brought in the car before heading back outside to direct the delivery of another piece of furniture.

The main hallway just inside the front door is tiled, with a nice wide staircase leading up to the second floor. I pause at the base of it, catching sight of Noah striding out of one of the bedrooms. He's on the phone again, this time with the locksmith as he organizes a time for someone to come change out our locks.

He makes a finger gun hand gesture at me as our eyes

meet, a tired smile crossing his face before he makes his way into the guest bedroom to help the movers there.

Finger guns are an inside joke between us. It stems from a story Noah once told me about the advice one of his friends gave him when he was at NYU himself.

Ladies love the guns.

Thankfully he never tried seriously to woo me with that ridiculous advice, but it cracked us up enough we still do finger guns to this day.

The silly gesture makes me smile despite the heat and the dehydration headache, and I turn around to step back out into the sunshine again.

I'm not sure how long this will take, but honestly, I'm eager for the sun to start going down so we can all get some relief from the blaze.

As I step back out into the yard, I see two people stepping onto our driveway from the street. It's a man and a woman who look to be about my age.

She's got blonde hair and is wearing a flowing summer dress, while the man sports an untucked white dress shirt and light grey khaki pants. Both of them are smiling, and they give a wave when they see I'm looking at them.

I wave back and then notice the woman is carrying something.

"Hey neighbor," the man says with another wave as they make their way up our driveway.

Now that she's closer, I see the woman is holding a plate of cookies.

"Hi," I say, slightly surprised but also delighted that they've come to introduce themselves.

To be honest, I was kind of dreading having to do the rounds. I've never been the most extroverted person, at least outside of a band performance.

That was acceptable in a place like New York, but I knew that once we moved out here, I'd have to switch it up if I was ever going to meet people and make friends.

Looks like I was worried for no reason at all.

"I'm Jenna, and this is Mark," the woman says. "We just had to drop by and say hello."

"Hi Jenna, Hi Mark. I'm Nikki, and my husband Noah is somewhere inside," I say with a hand wiggle at the house.

"Where are you coming from?" Jenna asks.

"The City," I say, and Mark nods knowingly.

"Us too. We love it out here so much more than Manhattan," he says.

Jenna nods in agreement and extends her arms to offer me the cookies. I'm shocked to see they look completely homemade, complete with little friendly *welcome*'s written on each one in frosting.

"Just a little something to welcome you to the neighborhood," she says.

"Wow, this is... thank you," I say, accepting the plate.

I can't believe she baked cookies on our account. Mark gives Jenna a side-hug as they stand in front of me, still smiling.

"Jenna is a wonderful baker," Mark says as he squeezes his wife again. "Her cookies are always the talk of the town at the block parties."

Jenna rolls her eyes, but it's clear from the color in her cheeks she adores the compliment.

"Mrs. Anderson?"

I turn my attention away from the couple and back to one of the moving guys, who's holding an end table meant for our bedroom between his arms.

"We'll get out of your hair, just wanted to wish you a warm welcome," Jenna says.

"Thank you again for the cookies. These are really wonderful," I say, waving goodbye to the pair before turning to go assist the mover.

How nice of them to stop by. As I head back up the driveway, a feeling of warmth moves through my chest.

We made the right decision coming here. No matter what happens from here on out, I know we'll have at least a couple of friends in the neighborhood.

At the door, I direct the mover with the end table upstairs with a shout to Noah to draw him out of one of the bedrooms.

"Make sure this goes on the left side," I say to him when he pokes his head out, and he nods.

The move-in is truly underway now, with me scurrying back and forth, dripping with sweat in the scorching hot afternoon sun.

"Excuse me."

I turn around to face the doorway, expecting to see another mover with a question about where to put something. Instead, it's another couple, both of them standing in the doorway with broad smiles across their faces.

"Hi there! I'm Aaron, and this is my wife, Helen," the man says, stretching out a hand.

A look down at Helen reveals a plate of what appears to be brownies in her hands.

"Hi. We just wanted to pop over and give you a nice welcome to the neighborhood," Helen says as she offers me the dessert plate.

I take it with a sweaty smile and a hearty thanks then introduce myself. We converse for a few minutes before they excuse themselves and leave.

Two movers are carrying a rolled rug through the doorway, so I wait another moment before stepping inside after them to put the brownies in the kitchen.

I can't believe another couple came to say hello. That's so wonderful.

No sooner have I gotten the fridge open than I hear a call from the open doorway, where yet another smiling couple stands.

They remain politely on the doorstep, giving me a wave as I spot them.

Incredibly, I catch sight of two more pairs of people walking over to the house as I stride back through the sparsely furnished living room, dodging the movers to make my way to the door.

There's so much happening at once, between the continual stream of neighborly introductions and accepting of gifts—not to mention the constant shouts and questions of the movers. My head is buzzing, and everything sort of begins to blur together.

It doesn't help that I'm exhausted, having gotten up early to pack, spent all day in the sun and heat, not to mention the harrowing drive through city traffic in our newly leased car to get here.

The cumulative effect is that I'm stressed out of my mind.

I find myself able to give little more than a smile and a nod of thanks as more and more couples arrive, popping up almost by magic to offer me some delicious dessert as the movers continually cross my field of vision.

By the time the final box is unloaded (full of Noah's vintage record collection), he and I are both absolutely wiped.

We're sitting on the couch now, though collapsed on the couch may be a more appropriate description.

Even Petey seems tired. He worked hard in his own way, barking for most of the day, "protecting" his people.

For the first time in hours, there's silence. No grunting, no questions, no more stress.

We've officially moved into our new home. Our new lives. I look over at Noah to find him already looking at me, a tired smile on his face.

"We did it," he says, before leaning over to kiss my head.

"The perfect house in the perfect neighborhood. And it's ours."

He pulls me into a hug, and I sink into his arms and close my eyes, breathing him in.

Cardboard boxes are everywhere, piled nearly to the ceiling in some places. There's still so much to do, but we're here now. We're really here.

"Still plenty to unpack," I say, my voice a little muffled.

"True, but still, I think we should celebrate," Noah says as he sits upright with a little effort.

"Luckily the wine made it here in one piece. Why

don't we crack a bottle and stay up all night like we used to?"

I let out a giggle. We haven't done that since we first started dating. I've got Petey to thank for that, actually. If he hadn't barreled into Noah in Central Park chasing a ball, we probably never would've met.

Since we didn't work together, the only time we could really see each other was in the afternoons and evenings, but we just couldn't get enough of each other's company and didn't want to stop hanging out even though it was bedtime.

I can't count the number of times we watched the sun come up, having spent the whole night just talking. I was exhausted most of those first few months, but I don't regret a second of it.

Noah and I push off the couch and head into our new kitchen, his arm around me before we split off for him to grab a bottle while I search for the box with the wine glasses.

"I can't believe how nice all the neighbors were. We'll be eating good for a month," Noah says with a chuckle as he eyes the dessert plates covering the countertop.

My eyes rove over the array to see what appeals the most. "I say we start tonight. What do you think? Cookies, brownies, or pie? Or all three maybe?"

Noah says something behind me in response, but I don't really hear him.

My focus is on something else.

I swallow hard, my heart suddenly beating a little faster.

"Noah."

He pulls his head out of the fridge to look over at me, wine bottle in hand. "Yeah?"

"Look," I say.

My throat is dry as I stare down at one dessert plate in particular.

"Fly in the food or something?" Noah asks as he comes up behind me. "Is—"

His words cut off as he sees it too.

The single word written in frosting across one of the cupcakes among a dozen others.

RUN.

THREE

NIKKI

Noah shakes his head as he gulps down the rest of his wine.

"It's a joke. It has to be. Right?"

It's late, and we're staying up like we used to, but tonight's celebratory vibe has been altered slightly by the strange word written in the frosting.

With as many new faces as I saw today, and as many plates as Noah and I accepted, I have no idea who gave it to us.

I take a small sip from my own glass, letting the wine swish over my tongue a moment before swallowing.

"Yeah. You're right. Has to be."

Noah nods to himself as he lifts the bottle and pours another glass. Even after his declaration, I can tell he's still a little off put.

"I'm trying to rack my brain to remember everyone that came by," he says. "And I didn't even meet all of them. Any idea who it could've been?"

I shake my head. "None."

I was on auto-pilot for a good couple hours there, thanks to the constant motion and stress. Noah shrugs and takes another sip of his wine.

"Well, I guess we've got a jokester on the block. Hardy-harr-harr," he says.

"Yeah," I say again.

An odd feeling I can't quite place has taken up residence in my chest. It's weird. Just a couple hours ago, I was firmly floating on cloud nine.

Perfect house, wonderful, welcoming neighbors, an exciting new beginning. And now there's this little knot of worry that I can't seem to shake.

It's a joke, I'm sure. Some wise-guy, like Noah said.

As much as I assure myself of that, there's still the tiny little voice in the back of my mind that can't help but wonder if it's not.

I take another sip of wine and chastise myself. *Don't be ridiculous.*

We're in the suburbs, after all, not the city. It's safe here, calm, peaceful. All the crime is back in the city— and that's part of why we left.

Noah's looking out the window, which draws me from my thoughts.

"What?" I ask.

He shifts a little farther down the length of the couch to get a better view between the parted curtains.

"I see someone out there," he says.

Setting my wine glass down on the coffee table, I scooch up beside him and peer out as well. We watch in silence as one of our neighbors carries an old wooden chair down to the bottom of his driveway.

I remember seeing him earlier, though I can't remember the name. Kevin? Mark? Andy?

They've all blended together in my mind.

He sets the chair down but remains there another moment, standing with his back to us.

"What's he doing?" Noah murmurs.

Then the man turns—and looks right at us.

He gives us a big wave. After a moment, Noah lifts his hand and does the same. Then the man heads back up his driveway. Noah takes another sip of wine.

I breathe out. We've gotten ourselves worked up over nothing. The neighbors couldn't be any nicer, we're super lucky.

It's just our big-city brains, conditioned to be battle-ready, that have us even questioning things in the first place.

"Let's see if we can get the TV going," Noah says, pushing off the couch.

He heads around the coffee table and over to our television, which the movers mounted but didn't plug in. Setting his wine glass on the mantle, Noah fiddles with the wires and fumbles around for a few minutes.

"Okay I think I got it," he says, grabbing the remote control and coming to sit beside me on the couch. "The moment of truth."

He points the device and clicks, and the TV screen blinks to life.

We both cheer, and I get up and go to the kitchen, returning with a plate of delicious-looking brownies that I set on the table in front of us. Then we settle in, snuggled up against each other on the couch. Our first night in the new home.

After signing into the various streaming services we pay for and perusing the options, we decide on a horror movie. I spend the next hour clutching tight to Noah, the two of us bursting into laughter as each of the jumpscares manages to get us without fail.

I don't know what time it is exactly when I drift off to sleep, but it's late.

My heart thuds in my chest as I jerk awake.

Squinting into the dark, I sit upright on the couch. Did I dream that noise, or was that real?

Petey lifts his head at my sudden movement, his eyes almost silver in the dark as he watches me from his little bed in the corner.

Noah shifts against me, his lips smacking together before his breathing returns to normal. He's still asleep. I must've just dreamed that rustling I heard.

Probably just new-house jitters, that's all. Totally normal.

The only source of light in the living room comes from the muted TV. It takes my groggy brain a second to parse through the action happening on screen. A hot girl is getting dismembered—some slasher film, auto-playing after we drifted off.

The light from the TV is thrown off in uneven bursts, illuminating swaths of the living room before plunging it back into darkness as the scene on screen shifts. A look over at the windows reflects the images back to me before allowing me to see outside when it goes dark again.

It's all quiet on the street. I swallow and settle back against Noah. Shutting my eyes, I take a few deep breaths in and out to try and reset myself. Just new house jitters, that's—

I bolt upright in tandem with Petey, whose attention is now firmly fixed on the back windows.

I definitely did *not* dream that second noise.

It came from the backyard.

FOUR

NIKKI

My heart leaps up into my throat as I shake Noah's shoulder, my eyes locked on the dark backyard beyond the kitchen windows.

"Noah," I hiss.

He mumbles something but doesn't pop awake. He had a couple more glasses of wine than I did.

Petey stands up in his doggy bed, a low growl rolling from his throat.

He heard the noise too. There's something in the backyard.

"Noah," I say again, my voice louder this time.

Noah cracks open an eyelid. "What? What's going on?"

"I just heard something in the backyard," I whisper, keeping my eyes on the windows.

I haven't seen anything, but I still don't want to turn away. My heart pounds against my ribcage.

"Okay? It's probably some little fox or something," Noah says, his eyes beginning to shut again.

A loud snap from the bushes wakes him right back up. Noah straightens instantly, and our eyes meet. His are as wide as mine must be.

Petey's growling loudly now and has moved out of his bed to put himself in between us and the back door. He's a brave little guy, that's for sure.

Noah swallows and slides off the couch.

"I'm gonna check and see," he whispers to me.

I reach out a hand to clutch his wrist. "What?"

"If it's a coyote or something, I want to confirm it so we can tell someone. Otherwise, I don't think we can let Petey out there in good faith," he says.

My eyes fall to the doggy door and its fabric flap. Petey growls again, all eight pounds of him standing very stiff in his defensive position.

Noah eases my hand off of him and creeps through the living room and back onto the tile that delineates the adjoining kitchen's dining area. Going to the wall of windows facing the back yard, he glances back at me once more before peering through the blinds.

I wait in the darkness, the seconds passing in sync with the pounding of my heart in my chest. Noah remains where he is, hardly moving.

"Anything?"

He doesn't respond, his face still pressed up against the window for another moment before finally letting his hand drop as he shakes his head.

"Nothing. Whatever it was, it's gone now," he says.

I nod. "Maybe we should cover up the doggy door until we know for sure."

"Good call."

He walks over to the kitchen table and picks up one of the moving boxes sitting beside it. With a grunt, he takes it over to the back door and drops it down in front of the flap.

"That'll do for now. Maybe we should get cameras for the yard, too," Noah says as he makes his way back into the living room.

Petey, who seems satisfied now that the situation has passed, saunters over to his bed and plops down.

Noah pulls his phone out of his pocket and winces as the light from the screen blasts his face.

"Yikes. At least tomorrow is Saturday, and we can sleep in," he says.

"I think you mean today is Saturday," I grumble, wrapping an arm around him as he lowers himself back down to the couch.

"Okay smartie-pants," he says, kissing me again as he gets himself situated to watch the next movie.

I'm awakened the next morning by the distant sound of a lawnmower. Gently I open my eyes, instantly regretting it as a beam of light coming through a crack in the curtains blasts me.

I let out a groan as the hangover headache settles into place. Guess it was still too early last night to feel it, but it's here in full force now.

Noah isn't on the couch with me. Rubbing an eye, I sit up and let out a yawn.

We left the windows cracked, and a wonderful summer breeze drifts in as I shift to put my feet on the floor. I hear the toilet flush, and then Noah emerges from the first-floor powder room.

His hair is sticking up at a funny angle from the way he slept on the couch.

"I'm definitely not in my twenties anymore," he says. His voice is a little hoarse from his own hangover.

I chuckle and run a hand through my hair, which must look as funny as his does.

"We live in the suburbs, and staying up all night is no longer fun—or even possible. I think we're getting old."

Stepping back into the living room, Noah opens the curtains, letting the full glory of the morning stream into the room.

He stands at the window, hands on his hips as he observes his new domain. I walk over to him, wrapping my arms around his waist and letting out another yawn. He rubs my shoulder.

Both of us look out at our new view in awed silence.

The front yard is amazingly green. The flowerbeds beneath our windows seem to pop with life. At the end of the driveway is the curved street of the cul-de-sac, with a small wooded area filling up the center. It's surrounded by a wooden fence that's been painted white.

All in all, it's just about perfect. Noah gives me another squeeze but then lets out a hacking cough that has me cracking up.

"Sorry. Kinda ruined the bliss, didn't I?" he says.

He rubs his face and lets out a breath. "Okay. What do we need to do today?"

The question serves to clear the sluggishness from my mind, my body snapping into go-mode.

"Groceries, for starters. Toiletries, cleaning supplies. We need to get these boxes unpacked, too. Plus the doggy door."

Noah nods through another yawn. "Why don't I take the car to the store and grab everything? Give you a chance to rest, since I know you did most of the heavy lifting yesterday."

I look at him, my chest warming. "Really?"

Noah kisses my forehead. "Just give me the list, and I'll be on my way."

"Thanks," I say, and I mean it.

After unpacking the bathroom box and retrieving our toothbrushes and face wash, we clean ourselves up and then Noah is out the door with a kiss goodbye.

"Text me if you remember anything else we need," he says before pulling the car door closed.

I stand in the front doorway, blowing him a kiss before stepping inside and shutting the door. There's a creak as the brakes of our car release, and then Noah eases it out of the driveway and back out onto the street.

I yawn again, rubbing my face. I'll be busy while he's gone—there's a lot to do to make this house a home.

I've only managed to take a couple steps down the tiled hallway when I hear a knock at our door behind me.

Did Noah forget something?

Turning around, I pad back up to the door and pull it open.

Standing there is a woman I don't remember seeing yesterday. She's older than Noah and me, maybe in her fifties with dyed blonde hair. Her bright smile is almost as blinding as the early-morning sun.

"Hi," she says.

"My name is Mary. Welcome to our little neighborhood."

FIVE

NIKKI

I smile and try to act like I don't have a pounding headache as I look at Mary.

"Hi, Mary. I'm Nikki. You just missed Noah, my husband," I say.

"I gave him a wave as he was pulling out," she says.

Then, "Oh! I know it looks like I didn't bring any sweets, but I did. I had my husband Ron bring them by yesterday."

I glance back at the large collection of desserts we now own piled high in the kitchen and think of the frosted *RUN*.

"That is so nice. Thank you," I say. "Sorry, yesterday was so hectic I could hardly keep anything straight. Which ones did your husband bring?"

Was she the one who did it?

"I made brownies," Mary replies, dashing my hopes.

"Did you try them?" she asks. "My daughter loves that recipe."

I smile, working to remain even-faced at the disappointment of not finding out the true meaning of the cupcake's message. It doesn't take long to get over it, because Mary's brownies really were fantastic.

"We did, actually. Last night. They were amazing, thank you."

Mary smiles again. "Good. That's good."

A moment of silence begins to stretch out between us as we stand there. Mary is still smiling. Everyone is certainly very pleasant here, that's for sure.

"You're coming from the city, I'd imagine," Mary says.

I nod quickly. "That's right. Noah will be commuting a few times a week. He works in shipping and logistics."

"Wonderful. Well, I just wanted to stop by and introduce myself to you, since I couldn't come by yesterday," Mary says.

She begins to turn around when I remember our early-morning adventure.

"Mary, have you had any sort of issue with coyotes or deer, or anything like that? We thought we heard something outside last night," I say.

Mary tilts her head. "Not that I'm aware of. You saw something?"

I wave off her obvious concern.

"No, just heard some commotion... I'm sure it was nothing. It's just that we have Petey here," I say, gesturing to Petey as I gently push him away from the door with my foot, "and I don't want him to get... gobbled up, you know?"

"Absolutely, absolutely," Mary says, nodding. "I can

ask around, see if anyone else has seen or heard anything."

"That'd be great, thanks," I say.

Mary smiles again. "Don't mention it."

She steps off the concrete stairs leading up to our door and starts back down the path toward the driveway.

"Oh—one more thing," she says, turning back to face me. "I know you two are still getting settled in, but we're hosting a block party tomorrow. Ron and I are in that one there."

Mary points off to the right at a house that's almost on the other side of the cul-de-sac. I can just make out a slice of it. The rest is obscured by the trees in the center. From what I can tell, Mary's lawn is absolutely immaculate, as is the shrubbery.

"Thank you so much for the invite, we'd be delighted to come," I say, smiling.

This is perfect. We'll be able to meet everyone and introduce ourselves and start to get to know our new neighbors right away.

Mary nods. "Wonderful. It'll start around three, but you are welcome to stop by anytime. And feel free to cook whatever you'd like."

"Three PM, sounds great. See you tomorrow then," I say with a wave.

I push the door closed as Mary starts down our driveway. Our first block party. A sense of giddiness rises within me as I pull out my phone to text Noah and share the news with him.

This is going even better than I could've ever imagined.

I had this vision in my head of everyone being closed off, of feeling isolated once we left the city, but it's becoming clear that isn't going to be the case. After yesterday's welcome and now this, I'm feeling more relieved and encouraged than ever.

The only slight issue is what to bring to the block party. I really don't do much cooking, and neither does Noah. Takeout was our go-to in NYC.

Now that we've got this great big kitchen, it would probably do me some good to learn, but with the party being tomorrow, I'll just get Noah to pick up something while he's out.

We want to make a good first impression, and I don't think giving our neighbors food poisoning would really do it.

I fire off another text to him, asking him to pick up some macaroni salad.

Whew, it's hot in here. The sun is high in the sky now, baking the world from above as I step back into the hallway in search of the thermostat that controls the central air system.

Turning it on, I let out a sigh as a blast of cool air falls down from the vent. Petey tags along at my heels as I move throughout the first floor and shut all the windows so the cool air doesn't leak out.

I move into the dining room and shut the first window in there, my hands resting on the sill a second as I look out at our front yard once again.

Perfectly green grass is bordered by a row of shrubs lining the edge of our property. They're dotted with lovely little yellow flowers. Below me, pink and purple hydrangea blooms catch my eye.

All of this is ours.

I step quietly through the dining room, my hand running along the length of the table as I go. I shut the window on the side, taking a moment to peer out that one at the side yard and the evergreen trees that divide our property from the neighbor's.

So much space. I've got a smile on my face as I move down the hall to the back of the house and the final three windows that are open in the living room. I shut the first, then the second.

We've got such a wonderful backyard. So much open space. Space that I can see happy kids running wild in a few years from now.

I grab the third and final window and pull down, still smiling as my imagination takes off. A sense of wonder fills me as I admire the lush planting beds against the back of the house.

I've never had anything like them in my life and can't wait to spend mornings with my knees in the dirt, watering and caring for the various plants and flowers.

Then I see the footprint in the mulch, and my smile falters.

SIX

NIKKI

Noah straightens up, his knees popping as he rises from the planting bed.

"It was probably one of the movers," he says.

A warm breeze blows across the backyard as the two of us stand there appraising the footprint in the mulch. I swallow, my fingers rubbing my throat.

"Back here? I don't remember any of them coming back here," I say.

Noah chews his lip. "Well, that's what it has to be, right? Maybe when they were taking breaks, one of them came back here for a smoke or something."

I let Noah's reasonable words wash over me. I guess that's a possibility. Yesterday was truly chaotic, and it's not like I had a firm grasp on everyone's location at every second of the day.

But still—the footprint is plainly there in the mulch, almost directly below one of the living room windows. I blink, my heart beating a little faster as I think of the noise from last night.

Noah seems to reach the thought at the same time as me. We turn to look at each other, eyes widening.

"You don't think..." he starts.

"I don't know what to think."

The behavior I've seen from our neighbors has been nothing but extremely warm and polite, and finding out one of them is a Peeping Tom would completely fly in the face of that. Still, we haven't met everyone yet.

Petey's barking pulls our attention away from the footprint for a moment as we refocus on the tiny dog racing through the yard.

"At least the king is pleased," Noah says.

Petey's doing laps through the grass, clearly a fan of having more room to roam. Back in the city, he spent far more time indoors than outside.

I watch him another second before looking back down at the footprint. My teeth chew at my lip, then I shake my head, willing away the worry.

Last night's noises and this footprint are simply a coincidence. It's not like we came back here and looked around after the movers left. It might have been left there before we even moved into the house.

Really, we have no idea when the footprint got there.

"Maybe I will swing by the store and pick up some backyard cameras today," Noah says.

"Just to be safe, you know? Can't hurt."

I nod. That prospect definitely sets me more at ease. We step back onto the patio and then head through the back door and into the house. Petey comes dashing in behind us, not wanting to be left alone.

He speeds off into the living room as Noah chuckles.

"Seriously, I think he's happier than we are to have moved in here."

Noah reaches into his pocket and pulls out the car key. "Okay, I'm going to head out again."

I pull him into a hug. "Sorry for freaking out a little there. I appreciate you turning around and coming back."

He shakes his head. "Not a problem. I forgot to bring water when I left, anyway."

We separate, and he once again heads off to the store. This time when I shut the front door, I throw the dead-bolt lock.

Releasing a sigh, I rub my temples to try and fix my thoughts. Petey looks up at me, his tongue hanging out of his mouth.

Once he realizes I'm paying attention to him, his tiny tail begins to wag.

"Okay. Want to help Mommy unpack?" I ask, to which Petey's tail wags even faster.

The two of us start in the dining room. It's a little alarming how much stuff we managed to accumulate without even realizing it over the course of only a couple years.

I spend the next hour slicing through packing tape and unwrapping various pieces of decor alongside plates and silverware. I know nobody has fine china sets anymore these days—at least not anyone my age—but these pieces belonged to my paternal grandmother.

She left them directly to me in her will because she knew how much I loved playing with them as a little girl when we'd have tea parties at her house. Since my mom left when I was really little, Nana filled that motherly role for me.

I take extra care unpacking the fine china, making sure that each piece is carefully placed into its position in the cabinet in the dining room corner. As I lift out the final stack of teacups, my phone begins to buzz in my pocket.

Emma starts talking as soon as I hit the button to answer the video call.

"So? You guys burn the place down yet or what?" she asks.

I smirk. "Hello to you too."

She's got her hair up in a bun and is wearing her glasses, having elected not to put in her contacts so far today.

"Yesterday was so boring without you here," Emma says. "It had to have been the first time we haven't hung out on a Friday since, what? Summer break Sophomore year?"

She's joking of course, though we do end up seeing each other multiple times a week. I feel a little pang in my chest as I realize that probably won't happen as often anymore.

"Everything was good though?" Emma asks sincerely.

"Move-in was good. We even got them to mount the TV for us," I tell her.

"Oh yeah, that's a big win. Give me the grand tour," Emma says with a gesture of her hand, wanting me to switch the camera around so she can see the place.

I giggle and oblige, turning the camera to give her a view of the dining room. Emma lets out a gasp.

"That's bigger than our dorm room was," she says.

"How about neighbors? Any crazy stories yet?" she asks as I bring her into the tiled entryway beside the staircase.

"Funny you should ask that," I start.

"Oh no," Emma says, her hand coming up to her mouth.

I quickly shake my head. "Actually, I take that back. Everyone so far has been amazing. But... we did find a footprint in the mulch around the windows this morning."

Emma's already shaking her head. "Nope. No way. If that was my house, I'm setting up turrets on every corner, hiring armed guards to patrol the grounds."

"Patrol the grounds? I live on a cul-de-sac, Em," I say with a chuckle.

"Exactly," Emma says, nodding. "You know how it is with those suburb-types. Bored out of their minds, nothing better to do but be nosy."

There might actually be some truth to that, though I'm still choosing to believe everyone I met yesterday really is nice and wouldn't do something like that.

"Maybe. We're thinking it was just one of the movers who left it," I say.

"Oh, yeah. Wait. Is it too late to cancel my order for a bulletproof vest and heavy machine gun?" Emma says.

I laugh. "Might be. But thank you for being willing to come to our aid, if need be."

Emma gives me a mock salute. "Anytime, comrade."

"What are you up to today?" I ask her.

"Let's see... Max and I are going to get brunch and

then take a walk around Central Park. Then there's this new Italian-Japanese fusion restaurant we'd like to check out, so we'll probably end up there," Emma says.

"You?"

I clear my throat. "Just uh, you know. Unpacking."

"Right. That sounds... fun," Emma says in a deadpan voice.

"Just kidding. *Loser*," Emma adds, drawing out *loser*, which makes me chuckle.

We say our goodbyes, and then Emma is gone, just like that. I'm alone again in a big house with no one but Petey.

Her day sounds like it's going to be fun and is probably something Noah and I would've done had we still lived in the city. But we don't, not anymore.

The most exciting thing on our schedule? This block party tomorrow.

I finish opening up the last of the boxes in the dining room as my mind drifts to the upcoming event. It'll be our debut neighborhood event as a couple.

Hopefully we make a good impression, because I'd really like to have some friends out here, considering everyone we know is back in the city.

I'm generally not one for nervousness, given the fact I used to play bass on stage like twice a week. Still, there's a little twinge in my chest as I think about tomorrow.

So many new people, all of them with expectations of some sort. If we mess up, it might spoil our time here.

Then again, all our neighbors are so nice, there's probably nothing to worry about.

SEVEN

NIKKI

Noah and I wake up early Sunday morning, having gone to bed early Saturday night. Both of us were wiped out after our movie session the night prior.

I feel well-rested today, my body fresh and renewed. Our mattress that we brought from the city is top of the line, by far the most expensive thing in our apartment.

Somehow, sleeping on it here felt even better. No weird noises last night either.

Noah lets me use the bathroom first, so I step inside and get myself ready for the day. I jam my toothbrush into my mouth and peer down into the backyard through the bathroom window.

Nothing but green grass and blossoming plants. After surveying our yard, I find my eyes roving over to the section of our neighbor's yard that I can make out. The height of the window allows me to see a slice of their backyard before being cut off by the fence.

Looks like they have a nice little patio setup, complete with a large fire pit in the center of the yard.

They must've just had a fire recently, because the pit is all blackened and surrounded by chairs.

How fun. Maybe if we impress everyone today, we'll be invited next time.

A little knock sounds at the door, pulling my attention away from the window.

"Honey, not trying to rush you, but I've got to pee pretty bad," Noah says through the wood.

I step over to the door and pull it open, toothbrush still between my teeth.

"We've got three bathrooms now, you know," I say, grinning.

Noah's eyes widen as he touches his forehead. "Oh my goodness, you're absolutely correct."

He marches out of the bedroom and down the hall to use the bathroom meant for the other two bedrooms on the floor to share.

"I am using our other bathroom," he declares triumphantly.

I pop my head back into the master bath with a giggle so I can spit out the frothy toothpaste.

Downstairs, we open the back door so Petey can race out and relieve himself. We're still using the box in front of the doggy door method, which isn't the cleanest look ever, but it'll do for now.

With as many other boxes still present down here, I don't really think anyone will notice. Plus, I'm not exactly expecting company anytime soon.

I follow Petey outside to keep an eye on him. Noah brings out two steaming mugs of coffee to join me on the patio, placing them both on the glass-topped patio table.

"Thank you, Mr. Anderson," I say with a smile as I look up at him.

"You're very welcome, *Mrs.* Anderson," he replies.

He settles into a chair as we take in the glorious morning sun. It feels incredible as it warms my face. Petey races around in front of us, tongue wagging as he darts from side to side across the yard.

Noah nods. "This is good. I like this."

It's a simple statement, but it expresses my feelings exactly.

Between the birds chirping overhead and the gentle breeze rustling my hair, this just feels... right. I reach over and give Noah's hand a squeeze. He squeezes back with a grin.

"I could definitely get used to this," I say.

I shut my eyes and lean back so my face is being warmed directly by the sun.

"Remember when we used to get woken up by Mr. Ralph's bugle practice at my old apartment?" Noah asks.

I snort. Mr. Ralph was an older gentleman who lived a floor above Noah in the apartment he lived in when we first started dating, on the Lower East Side. He played the bugle in a band some forty years ago, but still broke out his horn every Saturday morning at nine on the dot like clockwork.

"I much prefer waking up to the birds chirping, that's for sure."

"What time did Mary say the block party was?" Noah asks.

"Starts at three, but we can head over any time after

that. I get the sense it's one of those all-day drop-in things," I say.

Noah nods. "Sounds good. We can definitely get plenty of unpacking done before that."

Another day spent bent over the boxes. My back already aches a little from spending so much time yesterday hunched over them, sorting through piece after piece. The aftershocks of moving.

"What's Petey got?" Noah asks suddenly, bringing my eyelids back open.

I sit up a little, holding a hand over my eyes to shield them from the sun and give me a better view.

Petey's tiny body is hard at work as he digs away at something near the back of the yard. It had better not be a dead bird or mouse or something.

"Petey, no," I say, but he ignores me.

Clearly whatever he's found is much more important to him. Noah takes another sip of his coffee and then sets down the mug with a sigh. Both of us step off the patio and into the grass.

"Come on Petey," Noah says.

Nothing. The little dog remains entranced by his find. As we get closer, I realize he's not pawing around with something, he's actually digging.

Great. Now I'm going to have to add washing Petey's paws to the already long list of tasks for the day.

"Petey, wreck any more of my grass and you're sleeping outside buster," Noah threatens.

We come up behind him as Petey throws more dirt, his tiny paws burrowing down into the soil and tearing up the grass.

"Great," Noah says, throwing up his hands as he gets a first look at the carnage.

I squat down and gently nudge Petey aside. He wags his tail, little nose pointed at the ground.

"What did you find sweetheart?" I ask, already cringing in expectation of whatever animal corpse I'm about to stumble upon.

But as I move aside the dirt, I don't find a dead bird or a mouse.

Instead, I find two golden wedding rings stacked on a keyring.

EIGHT

NIKKI

My eyes find Noah's as his brow furrows.

"Are those..."

I nod as I push up from my squat. "Wedding rings."

My heart thuds as I hold the two rings in my hand. Specks of dirt and grass cling to the gold, smothering their luster.

"Why is there a pair of wedding rings buried in our backyard?" I ask with a large lump in my throat.

Noah shakes his head as he pushes them around my palm with a finger.

"Maybe they got lost?"

I look up at him. "I'd believe that if there was only one. There's two here, Noah. A pair."

My eyes are drawn down to the rings again. Even though they're just two circles made of gold, I feel the knot in my stomach return.

It's what this means. What it could mean for the couple who lived here before us. How could both of their rings have ended up back here?

"Do we know who was here before us?" I ask.

Noah shakes his head. "I can ask the realtor, maybe. Or the neighbors would know."

That's true. And we're going to a block party in just a couple hours. Everyone on the cul-de-sac will be there, which means someone is bound to know something about the home's previous occupants.

I close my fist around the rings, swallowing. Even though it's a pretty innocuous find, I can't help but feel slightly concerned.

It's definitely unusual, that's for sure. Noah and I head back over to the patio to finish our coffee.

"We can ask around at the block party, see if anyone has the number of the couple who was here before us. That way we can get the rings returned," I say.

Noah nods. "Good idea."

I don't mention the other thought that's running through my mind. The thought that wonders if something worse than just losing their rings happened to the couple before us. But we would've heard about something like that, right?

After coffee, we head back inside to make breakfast. I work on the eggs, while Noah pops some pieces of toast into our new toaster. We've got plenty of fresh berries too, thanks to his grocery trip yesterday.

I pull the pair of rings out of my pocket and place them onto the countertop. It doesn't seem like the proper place for them, but then again, I'm not sure what is.

Then the toaster dings, and breakfast gets underway. After we've eaten, it's time to get back to the business of unpacking and home organization. Noah connects his phone to a speaker so we've got some music to work by.

As soon as the first notes of soft piano jazz reach my ears, I feel a little better. We'll get the names of the couple who lived here before us and get their rings back to them.

Maybe they took their rings off for some project, and in the move-out, the keyring was lost?

That would make sense. I imagine them happily thanking us for returning their rings to them, and that makes me feel even better.

With the music to spur us onward, we make great progress on the unpacking. Noah pulls out our N&N candy picture. It's a spoof on the popular chocolate candy with our initials instead of the usual M's. Holding the framed picture, he dances on the tile and makes me laugh as he busts a silly move.

"Why're you laughing? You know you can't resist my dancing," he says.

He does a little spin and then props up an eyebrow, prompting another laugh.

Slowly but surely, the house is starting to come together. With the sheer amount of work there is to do, the time moves faster than I expected. By the time I glance up at the clock again, it's after two.

I place the last battery-operated candle on the windowsill and step back.

"What time do you want to head over?" I shout over my shoulder to Noah, who's in the dining room.

I hear his footsteps over the floorboards and then he appears in the kitchen.

"What's that?" he asks.

"What time should we head over?"

Noah shrugs. "I mean, we're in a pretty good place here to take a break, don't you think? Maybe we could shoot for three-thirty?"

"Sounds good," I say.

"Why don't you start getting ready, and I'll wrap up this last box," I add.

Noah heads upstairs to pop into the shower. Whenever we're going somewhere, he showers first since he's usually in and out within ten minutes. He is a guy, after all. I'll need a little more time, and I hate to feel rushed.

I hear the shower come on and dive back into the box in front of me. Petey gets busy ripping apart the little stuffed red fox toy he's had since he was just a puppy. It's hardly more than a few strips of furry fabric now.

We like to call it his "roadkill", because that's about the best description for it at this point.

A car rolls through the cul-de-sac out front, drawing my attention. It pulls through slowly, rounding the curve with care before arriving at the house two down from ours.

The car eases its way about halfway up the driveway and then shuts off. I see a man get out. It's Jenna's husband, from the couple that came over first.

We met yesterday, but I can't remember his name. It's either Adam or Mark, one of the two.

I guess I'll find out in a couple hours. A few minutes later, the shower turns off upstairs. Noah is out already, which means it's my turn. We're nearing three o'clock now.

After double-checking that the box is in place in front of the doggy door, I head upstairs.

It takes me a little while longer than Noah to get ready, considering I've got to shave my legs and my hair takes longer to wash. Once that's all settled, I step out of the shower with a towel wrapped around my body and head into the bedroom to sift through one of the cardboard boxes in search of something nice to wear.

Considering the temperature, I settle on a nice white summer dress with a floral pattern. Sort of similar to what I saw Jenna wearing yesterday. Noah's downstairs, making sure Petey has plenty of food and water for the time we'll be out of the house.

He lets out a whistle as I come down the stairs, making my cheeks redden a little.

"I think all the other guys at this party are gonna be jealous of me," he says with a wide grin.

"Oh stop it," I say, but secretly I love when he compliments me like that.

I make a quick stop at the fridge to pick up the tub of macaroni salad, and then we're saying goodbye to Petey as we head for the door.

As soon as Noah opens it, the distant noise of the party reaches us. There's music playing, though we're far enough away that all we can make out is the rhythmic pulse of the base notes.

I start down the driveway, macaroni salad in hand. Noah's wearing a plain blue button-down shirt untucked, with a pair of flowy linen pants and some sandals.

Laughter reaches our ears next, and my skin tingles.

Everyone here seems very comfortable with each other. I just hope we'll be able to fit in too.

It takes only a couple of minutes for us to walk down the street and up to Mary's front door. There are a few cars parked up against the curb from people who came from further down the street, and we weave our way in between them.

The noise of the party is much clearer now. I hear more laughter, followed by the shouts of children as they race around in the backyard. Noah and I reach the front doormat.

Written on it are the words *ALL ARE WELCOME.*

My eyes meet Noah's, and then he knocks on the door.

NINE
NIKKI

Mary's husband Ron opens the door, his face lighting up the instant he recognizes us.

"The Andersons! So glad you two could make it," he says, stepping out of the way for us to come inside.

The sounds of the party are even louder now. A quick look behind Ron shows an entry area similar to ours and a hallway leading to a kitchen in the back.

Unlike ours, their house is built into a hill, so the back deck is raised and has wooden stairs leading down to the yard. People are absolutely everywhere.

"—had to get some unpacking done," Noah is saying to Ron, who waves him off.

"You're just on time. We're just so happy you could come."

We follow Ron down the hallway, and he gestures to the left at a table with a bunch of little porcelain figures atop it.

"Careful of these. I think Mary might love these

things more than me," he says with a chuckle, giving the table a wide berth.

The hallway opens up into the main living room and kitchen area. The sliding back door onto the deck pulls open as Jenna's husband, who I saw getting out of his car earlier steps inside, a beer bottle in hand.

"Hey there, you two," he says.

Noah steps up and shakes the man's hand. "Hi, I'm Noah."

"Mark," the man says.

That was it. Mark.

He points to me. "And you're Nikki, right?"

I nod with a smile. "That's right."

Mark smiles back.

"I've always been good with names. Can I get you a drink, Noah?" he asks as he moves to the fridge.

"Sure, that'd be great."

I lift up the bowl of macaroni. "Where should I put this?"

Mark gestures to the counter, where a few other plates and platters are sitting. "Oh, just anywhere around there. Mary'll know what to do with it."

I plop it down and turn around to find Jenna standing there, a big smile on her face. She lets out a squeal and pulls me into a hug before I can even react.

"Hey neighbor! You're here."

"We're here," I say, surprised but not upset by the warm welcome.

"This is Noah," I say, and Jenna and Noah shake hands.

"How does—" Noah starts, but Mark's hand on his shoulder pulls his attention away.

"Come outside and meet some of the guys, Noah," Mark says, a broad smile across his face.

"Promise we won't rough you up too bad."

Noah gives me a quick look to check if that's okay. I smile to show him I'm all good here, so he allows himself to be led by Mark out onto the back deck.

"Let the boys hang out so we can get to know each other a little better," Jenna says, still smiling widely.

She has really nice teeth, I'll give her that. I guess I'd be smiling all the time too if my teeth were so white and shapely.

Jenna clasps her hands in front of her. "Do you want something to drink? There's some fantastic wine here."

"I think I'm okay for now," I say.

Jenna pauses by the fridge. "Are you sure? Everyone else has a drink."

She reaches for a bottle of red wine on the counter. "Have a glass."

I really don't want to drink much today, considering the excess of Friday night and that tomorrow is Monday.

Then again, Jenna's right. As I look around, everyone except a pregnant woman has a glass or a bottle in their hand. We want to fit in, right?

I feel like I'm back in high school again. I nod to Jenna, and she smiles again.

"Perfect. You're going to love this. Lewis's family—that's Melissa's husband—has a winery in Newport, Rhode Island."

Some shouting from outside makes me look toward

the window for a moment. Noah is standing among a circle of guys, all of them gathered around a grill that trails smoke into the afternoon air.

Jenna hands me the wine, turning my attention back to her. The deep red liquid sloshes around in the glass.

"Try it," she says.

I accept the glass and swirl it before lifting it to my nose.

"Rich taste," I say after a small swallow.

"Isn't it wonderful? We just can't get enough of it around here," Jenna says.

I nod politely and lower the glass again. Now that I'm here, my mind drifts back to the discovery of the wedding rings in the backyard.

"Listen. Did—" I start, but Jenna's grabbed my arm and is leading me toward the sliding doors.

"Time to say hello to everybody," she says as the sliding doors open to reveal another couple stepping inside.

"Hey Nikki," they say in unison.

Great memory. I blink, turning to say hello to them when Jenna pulls the two of us through the door.

"—are mostly in tech, though we do have a few people in real estate and finance as well," Jenna says.

I nod, only half listening. My eyes are roving around the backyard, taking everybody in.

Now that they're all gathered together, I notice how similarly dressed everyone is. I mean, it's actually quite remarkable.

Every guy I see is wearing a polo or dress shirt in some pastel shade, while the women all wear summer dresses in a similar fashion to mine. Sandals and boat shoes are the shoes of choice.

Looks like I made the right call not showing up in a ripped band tee. I remember Emma saying something about how Noah and I would become *suburbified* if we moved out of the city, and looking around now, I think I get it. It's practically a uniform.

"I want you to meet the girls," Jenna says, tugging me toward a group of women sitting in white Adirondack chairs set up in a loose circle.

My stomach does a little flip, so I take another sip of wine. It actually is pretty good.

Jenna and I approach the group.

"Ladies," Jenna says, drawing everyone's attention.

"This is Nikki Anderson. She just moved in."

I give the group a little wave, feeling my cheeks burn slightly at the sudden addition of a half-dozen pairs of eyeballs on me. How can I play bass in a bar in front of dozens of people but when it comes to a lawn party, I'm all frazzled?

"Hey everyone. I think I've met some of you, but things were pretty hectic, so apologies if I don't remember. Anyway, I'm Nikki. We just moved in down the street. I look forward to getting to know all of you," I say.

The group of women nod and smile.

"Glad to have you. Take a seat," one of them says, gesturing to an open chair beside her.

I lower myself into it, careful not to spill my drink on my dress and embarrass myself.

"I'm Denise," the woman who offered me the chair says with a welcoming smile.

There's a burst of laughter from up on the porch. Looks like Noah is managing to fit in.

"Clara," the woman on the other side of me says.

The rest of the circle sounds off their names, but again, there are so many and enough noise that I forget the rest almost as soon as I hear them.

"So, Jenna tells us you've moved in from the city?" Denise asks.

The rest of the group looks toward me with interest. I swallow and shift in my seat.

"That's right. We were on the Upper East Side, but finally decided we wanted a little more space."

A few knowing nods move across the group. Denise gives me a smile.

"I know the feeling very well. The city is no place to raise children."

I chuckle. "Actually, I grew up there, so I don't mind it all that much. But I get what you mean—and I'm certainly starting to see the allure of all this yard space."

Clara takes a sip of her wine, a big smile across her face.

"We're just so excited to have you here. It isn't everyday a new couple moves in," she says.

"Well, I'm glad to be here," I say, lifting my glass a little before taking a sip.

The rest of the group raises their drinks as well, and then finally the pressure is off, and I can let out a little sigh.

Seems like I passed the test.

"So," Clara says, giving my arm a nudge.

"How many kids do you think you'll have?"

I blink. A slightly odd question considering we don't know each other very well. Then again, Denise did mention New York not being a good place to raise children, so I suppose it isn't coming completely out of the blue.

"Um, I guess we don't have any concrete plans just yet. Though I think I would like to have more than one, you know? So they aren't lonely," I say.

Clara nods. "Two is a good number."

I think back to the two wedding rings we just found in our backyard as Clara starts to get up to refill her drink. Clearing my throat, I shift in my chair and say Clara's name to get her attention again.

"Hey, Clara. Did you happen to know the couple that lived in our house before us?"

Clara stops moving and looks back toward me.

"We just found their wedding rings in our backyard," I finish.

For the first time since I've met her, the smile drops off Clara's face.

TEN
NIKKI

It was only for a half-second, but I saw it.

I asked the question, and the smile faltered. I know I saw it, but now Clara's smile is back and almost bigger than ever as she shakes her head.

"I didn't know them, they mostly kept to themselves," she says.

"I think I'm going to have another glass. Would you like one?"

"No... thank you," I say, sitting back in my chair.

My brow furrows as I watch Clara walk away, her summer dress rippling as the warm breeze blows across the yard again. It carries with it the happy notes drifting from a speaker, along with titters of laughter and the clinking of glasses.

Despite her insistence, I have the distinct impression that Clara knew the couple. Or at the very least, knew more than she was letting on.

My question caught her off-guard, and that was why she stopped smiling for a moment before recovering.

But then why wouldn't she tell me? Why would she lie?

As the other women in the circle chatter away happily, I look down into my glass, swirling the wine in a slow circle. That strange interaction has left me with that tight feeling in my stomach again.

I swallow. Then I look over at Denise, who sees me looking at her and smiles.

"Enjoying the party?" she asks.

"Yes, thank you. It's been wonderful meeting everyone," I reply.

Denise nods and beckons me to stand with her. "Why don't I introduce you to some more folks? Come with me."

We step away from the chair circle and start back through the grass toward the house. I see Mary, the woman who invited me here, standing with her husband Ron near the grill.

She sees us and starts walking over, holding out her arms.

"Hi Nikki, so glad you made it," Mary says after giving me a hug.

"Thanks for inviting us," I say back.

"And you've tried some of the wine, I see. Good, good. Anything else I can get you?" she asks.

I give her a half-smile. "Actually yeah. I was just wondering if either of you knew the couple who lived in our house before Noah and I moved in. We just found their wedding rings in the yard, and I'd love to return them."

Denise and Mary both shake their heads, even before

I've finished speaking.

"I didn't know them," Denise says apologetically.

"They mostly kept to themselves," Mary adds.

I chew my lip. "Hm. Okay. That's kind of odd, right? I mean, it seems all of you made such an effort to include Noah and me and welcome us into the community."

Mary smiles. "We certainly tried. Can I get you another glass of wine, sweetheart?"

"I'm okay, thanks," I say.

"Well, if there's anything you do need, don't hesitate to ask me, okay? I want you to feel welcome here," she says.

Then she tells Denise and me goodbye before moving on to talk with other party goers.

That makes three people I've asked who didn't know the couple occupying the house before us. Very strange.

Denise threads her arm through mine. "Let's make a few more introductions, shall we?"

She directs me toward a small group of people, men and women who are all standing. I say my greetings and make small talk for a few minutes before my eyes rove around the backyard again in search of Noah.

We've been separated almost the entirety of the time we've been here, and I'd like to check in with him to see if he's been able to find out anything about the rings.

Where is he?

My pulse quickens slightly when I don't spot him on the first pass. Then I hear the sliding door pull open on the deck overhead, and the familiar timbre of his voice reaches me.

"—and logistics," I hear him say.

He's telling someone about work, the usual small talk at an event like this.

"And I just found out I'm having twins. Harry and I are so excited," the woman—Bridgette, I think it was—says.

I direct my attention back toward her and smile. "Congratulations, that's definitely something to be excited about."

"What about you and your husband? Have you two started trying yet?"

I slurp down another slug of wine. All of these people seem interested in the same topics. It's practically deja-vu over here.

"Not yet, no. I think we want to wait a few more years. Excuse me," I say, pulling away from Bridgette to head toward Noah.

I'm only a few steps away from him and about to call out his name when Ron steps over and wraps an arm around Noah's shoulder.

"Let me show you the garage," he says, steering him around the side of the house.

"I call it the man-cave, because it's the only room Mary'll let me decorate. You've got to see this mini-fridge I just..."

The two of them move around the side of the house before I can say anything. Great. Apparently I can't even talk to my own husband at this thing.

I take another irritated sip of wine, finishing my glass.

I've been sentenced to small talk with strangers for the foreseeable future.

Taking a short breath, I turn and face the backyard

again. Groups of people are scattered everywhere, all of them seeming to enjoy themselves immensely as they laugh and visit with each other.

I straighten my dress just to have something to do and try to decide which group to talk to next. One of the groups splits apart, allowing me to see through them to the base of the deck.

When they do, I see a woman sitting alone. Unlike everyone else at the party, she's not wearing a dress.

She's got on a cutoff band tee and jean shorts. Pair that with the piercings and the jet-black hair, and she sticks out like a sore thumb.

I can't help but watch her as she sits there, lighting a cigarette as the rest of the group seems to ignore her entirely.

I realize something else, too. Out of everyone here, she might be the only person I haven't seen before. Everyone else dropped off something at our house on move-in day.

Before I even really register what I'm doing, I'm making a beeline for her.

"Hi," I say as I approach. "I don't think we've met."

The woman takes a drag of her cigarette and then blows the smoke away from me. For a moment I think she's going to ignore me entirely, but finally her eyes slide over to me as she works her gaze up and down my frame.

"You're the new girl. Nikki," she says.

"That's right."

"Lily," the woman says before jamming the cig into her mouth again.

She's gruff and not smiling. Definitely doesn't fit in with the rest of this crowd.

Regardless, I plop down beside her on the bench. I'm not entirely sure why—maybe it's because of what she's wearing. Her whole look was basically me in college, which makes me think we'd get along, though it seems completely out of place at this party.

Lily seems slightly surprised but doesn't comment.

"So Lily...what do you do?" I ask.

"Nurse. You?" Lily says.

I shrug. "I used to bartend, though I just quit. I'm hoping to start writing some songs again, which I haven't done in a while."

Lily examines me for a moment, but doesn't respond. A few beats of silence pass between us, but it's not entirely awkward. If anything, I'm kind of relieved at the break from intensive small talk.

"I've got to admit, this is a little exhausting," I say while looking out at everyone mingling on the lawn.

Lily scoffs. "Better get used to it. Mary hosts these things every weekend."

"Every weekend? Well, I mean, it's not like it's mandatory or something," I say with a chuckle.

The pause before Lily speaks is long enough to make me look at her again.

"I guess not, no."

She takes another long drag of her cigarette before turning her head to blow the smoke away from us.

"Um... are you here with anyone?" I ask, just to break the silence that has descended upon us.

Lily jams the butt of her cigarette into the cement base of the bench with a shake of her head.

"I lost my husband," she says.

My hand comes up to my chest. "Oh my—I'm so sorry. I had no idea."

Lily ignores my apologies, instead centering her piercing blue eyes on me before she speaks again.

"Just be careful you don't lose yours too."

ELEVEN
NIKKI

I stare at Lily.

"What?" I ask, my throat tight.

"Look around you," Lily says with a nudge of her chin at the crowd.

I look at the joyous party happening around us, unsure of what exactly she's trying to point out.

"This place... it gets to people," Lily says finally.

"It'll test you."

I guess she means Noah and my relationship, but I'm not sure why.

From what we've seen, everyone and everything about the neighborhood has been extremely pleasant. I tell Lily as much, watching as she nods.

"Exactly," she says.

I'm not getting it. Lily shakes her head and then clears her throat as she pushes up to her feet. "Everyone here follows the rules. Fits in. Do the same, and maybe you'll be fine."

I gesture at her. "What about you? You don't look like you're making much of an effort at all. To fit in, I mean."

Lily shrugs. Definitely not much of a talker, unlike everyone else here.

"Just...keep your eyes open," she says.

Then she's walking off, leaving me to watch after her with the words of our odd conversation floating around my head.

Whatever the opposite of small talk is called, I think that was it.

What a strange conversation to have with a woman I just met. I stand up and amble back into the backyard.

"There you are—I've been looking all over for you," someone says from behind me.

It's Jenna. She's got two full glasses of wine in hand.

"There you go," she says, handing one off to me before I can protest.

She leads me away from the porch and back out into the yard. "You know, you should really join us for Book Club this week. We're reading this thriller novel I think you'd absolutely love."

"Thanks, I'll... I'll think about it," I manage, my mind still on Lily's words.

We arrive in front of a small group of women, including Bridgette and Clara from earlier. Jenna opens her mouth to say something when she's interrupted by Mary, who's moving toward us stiffly.

She's not smiling.

It almost looks as if she's upset about something, though it's such a foreign look for her face, I'm still a little confused.

Mary reaches our group and stops to lick her lips.

"So I was just inside," she says.

As I look around the group, everyone has diverted their eyes like guilty dogs.

"Who brought the macaroni salad?" Mary asks.

Her tone is harder than I've ever heard it before, and it takes me a second to realize she's talking about *me*.

Oh no. Was there something wrong with it?

My thoughts race—maybe someone had an allergic reaction, or it went bad overnight, though I refrigerated it as soon as Noah got back from the store with it.

"Was it you, Jenna?"

Jenna shakes her head quickly. "I made my bean salsa, Mary."

The rest of the group is completely silent, leaving me to hear only the pounding of my pulse in my ears. Gingerly I raise my hand, my throat dry.

"I brought it," I say in a small voice. "What's wrong with it?"

Mary turns toward me, her smile icy. "It's not home-made, Nikki. I asked you to *make* something for the party, remember?"

I swallow, my eyes darting around at the other women to see if this is some sort of joke. None of them are laughing. In fact, none of them will meet my eye, either.

"I... I thought you meant just bring something. I didn't realize you wanted me to make something," I say, stumbling over my words as I try to formulate a response.

All of this is so strange. Mary's acting like I've just

committed some heinous act, and the rest of the group is backing her right up.

To me, it's not a big deal at all. It's a macaroni salad.

"Sorry?" I add on top, not knowing what else to say.

My cheeks are tinged red. Why do I even feel embarrassed over something so stupid? I just moved in and have barely unpacked. And not everyone is a great home cook.

Mary gives me a close-lipped smile. "Can I talk to you for a moment, Nikki?"

The other women dissipate like smoke, leaving me alone with Mary within seconds.

"You like it here, don't you?" Mary asks me.

I swallow. "Yes."

She nods. "The reason why you like it here is because it's a nice place to live. It's a nice place to live because we all have respect for each other. When I asked you to cook something, to contribute to this block party, and then you show up with some store-bought prepared macaroni, I feel disrespected."

"Mary, I'm so sorry," I gush, "really, I just misunderstood you. I didn't realize it would be an issue—if I had, I never would've brought it."

Mary nods again.

"I'm glad to hear that, Nikki. Everyone around here likes you. It'd be a shame for you to do something like this again and mess that all up, don't you think?"

Before I can respond, she's already turned and started walking away from me. I stare after her, my cheeks still burning.

Did that really just happen?

I just got dressed down over a freaking macaroni salad.

Noah's standing with his back to me, so I come up behind him and loop my arm through his.

"There you are honey," I say, a pleasant smile plastered across my face.

"I think it's about time for us to be getting home, don't you think? Plenty of unpacking still to be done."

Noah polishes off his beer and sets it down. Then he extends a hand to the man across from him.

"Great to meet you, Dan. I'll definitely take you up on that offer to watch the game," he says.

We wave goodbye to the others in the small group before ducking away.

"What's wrong?" Noah asks in a quiet voice.

He can tell something has happened, either from my expression or my demeanor.

"I'll tell you when we're home," I say under my breath.

Mary and Ron appear in front of us.

"Going so soon?" Mary asks, her voice once again dripping with sweetness.

"Gotta check on our dog, and we still have a lot of unpacking left to do," Noah says with a chuckle.

"Thanks again for hosting us, this was great."

Mary smiles pleasantly at him, but I notice doesn't look at me once. Can she still be that miffed by the macaroni thing?

It feels like it takes another ten minutes just to get back into the front yard with all the goodbyes and well wishes from every single person in our path.

By the time we finally round the corner of the house, I feel thoroughly exhausted. The noise from the backyard party is muffled by the house as we walk away, allowing us to speak once we reach the edge of Ron and Mary's yard and step onto the pavement.

"I'm so glad you grabbed me when you did. That guy, Dan, would not stop going on and on about his brand new flatscreen," Noah says, rubbing his face.

We hold hands as we walk back around the circle toward our house. My dress blows around my legs as the late afternoon sun shines down overhead.

"So what happened? You did not look happy back there," Noah says.

I chew my lip and glance over my shoulder before I speak. I don't know what I'm expecting to see—Mary peering through one of the windows or something maybe —but the house looks normal. The sounds of the party continue just as before.

"You know that macaroni salad we brought? Mary got all worked up at me because it was store bought," I say.

Noah's eyebrows come together. "So what?"

"Exactly, that's how I felt. She told me she felt disrespected by it because it wasn't homemade. You would've thought I kicked her dog or something," I say.

Noah chuckles. "People in the suburbs don't mess around when it comes to these potlucks, I guess."

I lightly bat his arm. "I'm serious. I'm worried now that we've somehow soured ourselves to the rest of the group."

"Over some macaroni?"

"You didn't see her like I did," I say, wringing my hands.

Noah sees that I'm obviously a little distressed and slips his arm around my waist.

"We're fine. It's one little mistake. I'm sure she'll get over it," he says.

"Yeah," I say, biting my lip.

We walk past Jenna and Mark's house. They've got the blinds open and a light on in the living room, allowing me to see into their home as we pass. The interior is clean, with a blue and green color scheme. I look away.

"Did you manage to learn anything about the couple who moved out of our house?" I ask Noah.

He shakes his head. "No, and I asked a bunch of people. Seems like whoever they were, no one really knew them and they mostly kept to themselves."

I stop walking. Noah looks back at me. "What?"

"That's exactly the description I got out of everyone I asked, too. That no one knew them, and they kept to themselves. I mean that exact wording, in that exact order."

Noah's brow furrows again. "Now that you mention it... I feel like Mark might've said that verbatim. *I didn't know them, they kept to themselves.* That's what he said. I remember it because it almost seemed like he was reciting a line, or something."

I snap my fingers. "I thought the same thing when Clara said it! Why wouldn't they want us to know about them?"

"No idea. It's weird though, considering they're all so

eager to know everything about us. I must've been asked a half-dozen times when we're gonna have kids."

I feel my chest tighten as a chorus of laughter rises up from behind us. We're nearly to our driveway now, the sun just beginning to sink in the sky. Reaching it, Noah and I look back toward the party house in silence.

Just what kind of neighborhood have we moved into?

It's Monday, which means Noah needs to go to work.

I wake up when he does, thanks to his phone's alarm buzzing on his nightstand. Noah staggers out of bed and heads toward the master bathroom. I hear the door shut and see the light flick on, and then I'm back under again.

When I wake up to my alarm an hour later, the room is empty. Noah's already taken the car and driven to the commuter train station. With a yawn, I sit upright and tap my screen to shut off the shrill alarm.

Rays of sunlight seep into the room around the edges of the blinds. I push off the covers and step over to the window to raise them. Light streams in, making me wince at the solar assault before I'm able to adjust my eyes and look out over the street.

It's as quiet as ever, save for the distant sound of a lawnmower and a leaf blower. The theme song of the suburbs. I let out another yawn as I run a hand through my hair and make my way to the bathroom.

Once I've gotten myself ready for the day, I step out and pull on some shorts and a tank top. Yet another day of unpacking awaits me. My back begins to ache just thinking about it.

I come downstairs to find an excited Petey at the base of the steps. He's practically doing flips, he's so happy to see me. It puts a smile on my groggy face.

That's one of the many things I love about dogs. They're always ecstatic to see you again, no matter how many hours, minutes or seconds it's been since you last saw them.

"Good morning sweet boy," I say, reaching down to give him a pet.

Petey's tail whips back and forth with excitement as he lets out a little yelping bark.

Noah already put some food in his bowl this morning, so that's all set. I look across the empty kitchen. The only evidence that Noah was here is one of the cabinets being slightly ajar from where he took out his cereal.

A love of kid's cereal is one of Noah's quirks that I adore. He's a grown man in his late thirties with a full-time job in New York City, but he still does certainly love a nice bowl of sugar in the morning.

I put some slices of bread into the toaster and turn on the coffee pot as another yawn makes its way through me. When my eyes open again, I look out the kitchen windows toward the backyard.

I don't think I'll ever get over the thrill of looking out at such luscious green grass. In fact, I think I'll have breakfast out on the patio this morning.

Petey's tail wags excitedly as he stands beside the

back door. I balance my plate in the crook of my arm while I unlock it and pull it open with a drink in my other hand.

The tiny dog shoots into the yard, bounding across the open space with reckless abandon. I take a seat on the outdoor couch and let the warmth of the morning sun heat my skin. It feels absolutely perfect out here now, though I'm sure it's going to be another scorcher this afternoon.

A good day to spend inside with the AC blasting. Nibbling on the toast, I glance up at Petey before checking my phone.

Emma texted me a couple times. One is a picture of her with a frowny expression as she stands in front of our old building.

The other is a poop emoji. Business as usual.

I text her back with a poop emoji of my own, followed by a *miss you* before diving into breakfast. After I'm done, it's time to get to work.

Petey and I head back inside, and I dive into the cardboard boxes, my speaker playing hard rock tunes as opposed to Noah's jazz. I was raised by my dad after all, which means I grew up on rock and roll. With my head bobbing, the day moves quickly.

I stop for a quick lunch, and then it's right back to it. It feels like the next time I look up, Noah's car is pulling into the driveway. My phone says it's half past six. Wow, those hours really flew.

As I stand up and wipe the sweat from my brow, I can actually see the hours of work reflected in the house around me. It doesn't seem like some empty, lifeless box anymore.

The living room and kitchen are basically done, which means all that's left are the boxes on the upper floors.

I hear keys jingle and then the front door open, Noah stepping through a moment later with a smile on his face.

"Well hello Mrs. Anderson," he says, his eyes going wide as he gets a look at the place.

I go up on my tiptoes and kiss him, even though I'm a bit of a sweaty mess. Together we head down the hall into the kitchen.

"How was the commute?"

Noah sets down his briefcase on the counter. "Not bad, really. Train ran smoothly, no issues. I could get used to this," he says, giving me another kiss.

He steps over the fridge and pulls out a frozen power bar for a snack. "Looks like you had a great day around here, too."

"We can almost officially say we're moved in," I declare with a tired smile.

It does feel good though, and I didn't mind the solitude at all. I needed a day to regroup and recover after all the "peopling" yesterday.

Noah rolls up the sleeves of his dress shirt. His office is business casual, which means no suit, although I think he looks great in them.

"I'm gonna pop into the shower, and then I think we're due for a movie night," Noah says.

He pushes away from the countertop and toward the tiled hallway again.

"What are we thinking, scary movie? Action?" he asks.

"I vote for a rom-com," I say with a giggle.

Noah rolls his eyes. "Okay, but only because I love you. And if you promise to watch that thriller *Vivarium* with me at some point."

I chuckle. "You got yourself a deal, mister."

Pouring myself a glass of water, I plop down on the couch to find a movie as Noah rounds the corner of the stairs. He makes it three steps up before pausing and leaning over the bannister.

"By the way, where'd you put those wedding rings we found? I wanted to take a picture to send to the realtor," he asks.

I nudge my chin toward the kitchen without looking back at him, my focus still on the TV as I sift through our romantic comedy options for the evening.

"Right there on the countertop, remember?"

"Yeah, but I mean after that. I just checked and they weren't there," he says.

I put the remote down and turn so that I'm facing him.

"What?" I ask.

Noah nods. "Just now, I just looked. They aren't there."

I swallow and blink. "I haven't touched them."

Noah straightens a little. Now it's his turn to be confused. "What?"

My head is shaking as I push off the couch.

"I didn't move them."

He jogs back down the stairs, coming up behind me as the two of us enter the kitchen. Just as he said, the two wedding rings are no longer there on the countertop where I left them yesterday.

My throat tightens as I stare at the empty space on the counter. Noah tilts his head slightly.

"If I didn't move them... and you didn't move them... where did they go?"

THIRTEEN

NIKKI

I push off my knees to rise out of a squat.

"They didn't fall beneath the counter," I say with a shake of my head.

Noah pulls open the first drawer and then pauses.

"Nikki," he says.

I take a step over to him and peer down into the drawer. Inside are the two wedding rings. Noah scoffs and shakes his head.

"Whew, you kinda had me rattled there for a second."

I continue to stare at the rings, my heart pounding in my chest. I didn't put them in there.

"That wasn't me," I say.

Noah looks over at me.

"Are you sure? You've been in and out of here all day hauling boxes and everything. Maybe you just tossed them in there to clear up space?"

"Maybe..." I say, but I think I'd remember.

I guess it's a possibility. I really did kind of zone out

for a while there, after all. The hours flew by without any conscious recognition. I suppose I could've just swept them off the countertop at some point without even realizing it.

Noah leans down a little to find my eyes.

"Hey. You okay? Sorry if I sounded kinda accusatory just then. I didn't mean to, I just wanted to figure out how the rings moved, because if you didn't do it..."

He trails off.

"I don't even know," he finishes, throwing up his hands.

"Look at us. First week in the suburbs, and we're already losing our minds," he adds with a chuckle.

"All this moving stuff does have me a little scrambled," I say. "I'm sure I just tossed them in there without thinking."

I decide it's the only logical explanation.

Noah nods. "Right, yeah. That makes sense. I mean hey, I was half asleep this morning getting ready for work. Maybe I moved them and just don't remember."

I notice his eyes flick over to the french back doors that lead out onto the patio, though. It's just a single step away from the counter where the rings were.

"Let's be double sure that's locked tonight."

If someone did come in and move them, the question then would be why? If someone was in here, I'd think they'd want to take the rings, not just move them around.

I must've just moved them. Or Noah did while he was still waking up. That has to be it.

Both of us are just overthinking this, still a little

scrambled from the move in. It'll take a few days for us to settle, I'm sure.

Noah heads back upstairs to take a shower, while I return to the couch. Petey leaps up with me, burying himself in my lap the moment my rear hits the cushions. I hear the bedroom door close upstairs as Noah gets undressed.

It's still light out, given it's summer, but I can't help but feel a little jumpy regardless. More than once, I find my gaze pulled toward the counter, and then to the back door and windows. The blinds provide only a choppy view of the backyard beyond.

One of us moved the rings. No other option makes any sense.

After Noah's done showering, I head up there and wash the sweat off me. Stepping out of the shower, I find myself drawn to the window. The daylight has almost completely faded by now, darkening everything outside.

I look down into the section of our neighbor's yard that we can see. It's Clara and Bill's place. Almost on cue, the back door opens, and Bill strides out.

He stops at the edge of his patio, standing there with his shoulders heaving like he's trying to recover his breath as I watch, the bathroom thick with steam around me. With his back to me, it's tough to figure out why he's breathing so heavily.

Just had a workout, maybe? Breathing exercises?

After almost a minute, he promptly turns around and heads back inside. I towel off the rest of my body and rejoin Noah on the first-floor sectional.

We watch the movie and then make a quick dinner of

rice and vegetable power bowls together. By the time the sun sets, I see Noah starting to yawn. With the hour commute into the city, he's got to get up around six-thirty to be in by nine.

We call it a night just after ten, kissing each other and then turning off the lamps on our respective bedside tables. I hear Noah put on his mouth tape and then settle into place, going still beside me.

As much as I'd like to drift right off, I'm not really all that tired yet. I got up later than Noah did, plus I can't stop thinking about those wedding rings.

About how everyone I spoke to at the block party seemed adamant about avoiding the subject. Then having the rings move today, whether it was us or not... it's all odd.

Within minutes, Noah's already breathing deeply, sound asleep. The one benefit of working hard five days a week. He can fall asleep practically standing up, while I'm left to my thoughts.

I turn over in the bed, careful not to shake the mattress too much so I don't disturb Noah. It seems like no matter how I position myself, though, I still can't seem to get comfortable.

Letting out a sigh, I slide out from underneath the covers and put my feet on the carpet.

Noah continues to snooze away peacefully, completely undisturbed. I reach for my phone and lift it off the charger.

The brightness of the screen makes me wince a moment before my eyes adjust, and I take a few steps to the bedroom door and step out so that I won't risk waking my husband.

Emma answers my text within seconds.

Of course I'm up. Life in NYC really only gets fun after 11, you know this, she says.

I can't help but smirk. Despite the fact we're in our third decade of life now, Emma still hasn't given up the party. At this point, I'm not sure she ever will. I would've said I could never see her moving out to the suburbs like me, but then I think of Lily, the rocker girl from the block party.

Everything ok??? Emma texts.

Fine, I text back, *just some growing pains in suburbia. Noah and I also might be losing our minds.*

Well that's nothing new Ki, Emma jokes.

Very funny. I miss you, I text back.

Miss you too. Maybe I come up this weekend?

I smile at my phone. *That would be great.*

My new neighbors seem nice enough, if a little odd. While I could make some new friends, I definitely don't foresee myself getting as close with anyone here as I am with Emma.

Except maybe Lily, though she didn't appear all that receptive to striking up a friendship. Then again, she did warm up a little the longer we talked, so maybe there's something there.

In any event, I can't wait to see Emma. It hasn't even been a week yet, but with all the major life changes happening around me, it feels like a lifetime. I could definitely use a night where it's just me, her, and a large bottle of wine.

Something clatters outside, bringing my head up. I'm in the carpeted hallway, the bedroom door slightly ajar behind me. Noah rolls over in bed as I creep back inside and move to the windows at the front of the house.

The street is dimly lit by a few light poles scattered around the cul-de-sac, though they don't provide much light. I stand silently, phone still in hand as I watch the night.

Must've just been some little animal or something, and—

Two people emerge from the shadows. They take a few steps forward and then stop.

They're standing completely still now.

Completely still in front of our house.

FOURTEEN
NIKKI

Though it's dark in the bedroom, I duck down out of instinct.

My chest throbs as I hunch there, blinking hard. I didn't just imagine that, did I?

I push up a couple of inches, so that my eyes are just able to see outside over the bottom of the windowsill.

The two people are still there. I can just barely make out their silhouettes in the weak glow of the streetlights.

They're standing almost in the middle of the road, their identities cloaked in darkness. It's definitely a man and a woman, given the height difference, but that's all I can make out. I guess that's part of getting older right there—my eyes just aren't what they used to be.

I swallow hard. Squinting doesn't do much to improve my vision—it's just too dark out there to see who it is.

My heart pounds. What are they *doing*?

The way they're just standing there, stock still, there's

nothing to think other than that they are watching the house.

I continue to stare down at them, afraid to move now in case the movement somehow draws the pair's attention. They still haven't shifted from their position.

For the life of me, I can't figure out what they're doing. The three of us remain frozen for nearly another minute. And then just as suddenly as they appeared, the pair starts walking again.

My eyes trail after them. They're walking down the road to our right—and then they stop again. Now they're standing outside our next-door neighbor's house, watching that one.

What in the world?

All of this is so strange, I don't know whether to be freaked out or what. I almost want to wake Noah up but then think better of it.

The couple is moving again. They've spun around so that they're marching into the forested circle in the center of the cul-de-sac.

As dark as it is, I lose them within seconds between the shrubs and the trees. All of it was so surreal, I'm still not entirely sure it actually happened.

Was it some type of neighborhood watch? Or just an extra-nosy couple taking a late-night stroll?

I have no idea. If only I'd been able to make out who they were.

As I slip into bed again, I add the couple to the list of oddities we've encountered so far since we've moved to the neighborhood.

I WAKE up the next morning to the already-familiar sound of a lawnmower.

There must be some sort of competition around here for the best grass, because it seems like there's someone working on their lawn every day of the week.

Noah's already left for work. I didn't even stir when he got out of bed. Guess I was in a pretty deep sleep. Today is Tuesday, and I'm going to make it the final day of unpacking.

Once that's finally off my plate, I think I'll be able to breathe easier and think more clearly.

I shuffle downstairs, stifling a yawn as Petey greets me with his usual ecstatic excitement.

"Good morning sweetheart. Did Daddy feed you?" I ask.

I peer into his bowl, where a small pile of dog food sits.

"He did. Good job, Daddy," I say with another yawn.

Padding my way into the kitchen, I pause as my gaze falls to the drawer where the rings were yesterday. Licking my lips, I pull it open—and then let out a breath of relief.

They're still there. Shaking my head, I make my way to the coffee machine.

Today doesn't appear to be as sunny as the past few days have been. I peer up at the sky, noting the plump grey clouds in the distance.

"Might get a little summer storm, Petey," I say over my shoulder.

This is bad news for Petey, who is deathly afraid of thunder. No judgment. I think if I weighed under ten pounds, I'd probably be afraid of the sky shouting at me too.

Better let him get his energy out now then, before things get yucky outside. As soon as I get the door cracked open, Petey shoots out like a bullet.

I join him outside, the humidity instantly making me feel like I've just stepped out of the shower. Once my coffee is finished, we head back inside to make some breakfast and then get started on today's unpacking.

Plenty of boxes still to take care of upstairs, and I get right to it.

Petey joins me, happily tearing apart his roadkill on the carpet beside me as I work. I've got my speaker blasting rock again, and it makes the time fly. With the music as a backing track, the work moves easily. I'm an unpacking machine.

I lift my head and cock it to one side, listening. Did I hear someone knocking at the door?

I'm not even sure what time it is—I've been in that timeless unpacking zone. I know at least a couple of hours have passed as I've worked steadily.

The sky outside is a lot darker than it was this morning, though I don't think it's started raining yet.

My head sweeps back and forth as I search for my phone to turn the music down. There it is, over on the guest bed. I shake out my sweaty t-shirt and then grab hold of my phone, turning the music down below ear-scorching level as I listen again.

Knock-knock-knock.

Definitely someone at the door.

Hustling out of the spare bedroom, I start down the carpeted stairs, dabbing at my face with my t-shirt to try and clear some of the perspiration. It's probably the locksmith, here to switch the locks on all the doors.

I pull open the door, but instead of the locksmith it's Jenna, who's standing there with a wide smile.

"Hey neighbor," she says brightly.

"Oh, hey," I reply, feeling a little self-conscious at my slightly disheveled appearance compared to Jenna's put-together look.

She's wearing a full face of makeup with an ironed dress and matching headband. Very chic.

"Hope you're doing well. I just wanted to pop by and invite you to Book Club tomorrow evening with me and some of the girls," she says.

"Oh, that would be great, thanks," I say in a rush.

Looks like the macaroni snafu has not completely alienated me, thankfully. Jenna nods and beams.

"Come by Mary's at about eight, okay?"

I blink.

"Oh. It's at Mary's house," I say.

"Yep! Mary's sort of the ringleader around here, you could say. But if you're concerned about the block party thing, no biggie," she says. "Mary understands it was all a misunderstanding."

"Okay," I say, feeling slightly less excited about Book Club now, "I guess I'll see you tomorrow at eight."

Jenna doesn't immediately respond, and it pulls my eyes away from the street and back to her face. She quickly readjusts her gaze to me and smiles again, but I could've sworn she was looking past me into the house, or something.

"Fantastic. You're going to have so much fun," she says.

"See you then," I say, beginning to shut the door.

More and more I'm starting to get the impression that Jenna is a little strange. She's always smiling and happy, yes, but it almost seems... phony. Like some sort of cover. A blanket thrown over something to obscure what's underneath.

Then again, I've known her less than a week. Maybe she really is this overjoyed about every little thing. I close the door, but for whatever reason, don't step away from it.

Instead, I peer through the foggy glass panels on the right side of the door and watch Jenna as she starts back down the driveway. I don't even know what I'm expecting to see.

Maybe I'm still a little spooked about that couple I saw walking around last night. Now that it's daylight however, I'm sort of viewing what I saw differently. It was two people taking a walk, probably.

They might have stopped to talk about the new neighbors that moved in, and that's why they were standing in front of the house for so long. That doesn't entirely explain why they stopped in front of the house next door too, though.

I head back upstairs to continue with the unpacking but only make it through another half of a box before the doorbell rings. This time it is the locksmith, who doesn't seem to be one for pleasantries as he grunts his way through introductions before getting to work.

Once he's finished, I'm left alone with Petey once again. It's started to rain now, and I turn down the music so that I can hear the gentle patter of the droplets against the windows. I've always loved the sound of rain, ever since I was a little girl.

I stand there by the windows with a small smile on my face as I think back to telling Dad all I wanted for Christmas was a sound machine. That was probably the only time in recorded history a parent has asked their child to ask for something *more* for Christmas.

There's just something so... safe about rain, I guess. That's the only way I can phrase it. Maybe it's knowing that if you can hear it, that means you're inside where it's warm and dry.

Standing by the window, I see Noah's headlights as he drives down the street toward our house. A few minutes later, he's inside, shaking off a few raindrops from his hair as he greets me with a kiss.

"Hello Mrs. Anderson," he says with a grin.

"Hello to you, Mr. Anderson," I reply.

"All quiet on the home front, I hope," he says as he sets his briefcase down on the countertop.

"Locksmith come by?" he asks as he dives for the fridge.

"He did... Jenna also came by. I've been invited to Book Club tomorrow."

Noah spins around. "That's great! See, I told you it'd all work out. Nobody gets permanently ostracized over some macaroni."

I chuckle. I guess he's right. I was overthinking everything, probably because I want so badly for us to fit in and for everything to work out here.

Now that Noah's back, the time seems to fly by, as it always does when we're together. Before I know it, it's time for bed.

Unfortunately, it's a repeat of the night before. I'm lying awake staring up at the ceiling while Noah sleeps peacefully beside me.

The next morning comes and goes as usual. We've fallen into a routine now. Noah gets up for work, heads downstairs to feed Petey and himself, and then he's out the door. I get up a little later and come downstairs to do a little cleanup after him.

With the packing done now, there isn't a whole lot more to do for the new house besides pick up a few things at the store to round everything out. This place is much bigger than our apartment in NYC was, so there are some rooms that seem a little bare.

I order a ride to the store and back, and spend the afternoon moving things around, trying to find the perfect locations for our new décor. Before too long Noah's pulling into the driveway again.

We kiss as he enters then spend a few minutes talking about our respective days. I've decided I'm going to make something to bring to the book club, as a sort of apology to Mary.

It takes a few minutes to decide on a fitting recipe, until the perfect idea hits me—macaroni salad.

I spend about a half hour preparing it, and then it's time for me to head over to book club. I go into the fridge and pull out the homemade macaroni salad.

"I'd guess I'll be about an hour? Not really sure," I say as I double-check my hair in the hallway mirror.

Noah pulls an arm around Petey who's happily ensconced on the couch beside him. "Then it'll be guys night, right Pete? We'll have a few beers, maybe invite some girls over."

I roll my eyes and adjust the plastic wrap across the top of the macaroni. "Very funny. Okay, I'm headed over. Love you."

"Love you too," Noah calls from the couch as I pull the door shut behind me.

Today was another rather rainy day, though it began to taper off in the afternoon. The only sign of the downpour now is the shiny puddles and slick grass around me as I head down the driveway toward the street.

The sky has begun to fill with a beautiful shade of pinkish-purple that has me walking extra slowly and craning my neck to gaze up at it. Then my phone buzzes, snapping me out of it. I don't want to be late for Book Club.

While I was out today, I picked up a copy of the book we're reading, a thriller called *The Housemaid* by Freida McFadden.

We're discussing the first ten chapters tonight, which is why the non-decorating part of my day was spent reading so I'd be able to contribute intelligently to the conversation. I ended up finishing the whole thing in one go. I just couldn't help myself.

As I walk around the cul-de-sac, I find myself peering into the cluster of trees in the center where I saw the couple walk through a few days back.

Of course now, it's just branches and leaves. I continue walking with the book underarm and macaroni in hand, coming up on Mary's house within another minute.

Walking up her driveway, I can't help but peek at the lit windows a little. I can just make out the hubbub of conversation from inside, but don't see anyone. Swallowing hard, I come to a stop in front of the door.

Time for a do-over. A second chance to ingratiate myself here.

With a deep breath, I knock.

FIFTEEN

NIKKI

The door swings open to reveal Mary standing there, her blonde hair perfectly straightened.

"Hi Mary," I say, already feeling my heart beat a little faster.

Holding out the macaroni container, I say, "I made this myself—it's homemade. Again, I'm so sorry about—"

Mary cuts off my apology, accepting the dish with a smile. "That's very sweet of you, Nikki. Thank you. Come in, welcome. And you brought the book too, I see. Off to a good start here."

I smile happily. Bringing something homemade over was absolutely the right move.

The hallway fills with noise as the rest of the women come forward, everyone saying hello and welcoming me. Some even pull me in for hugs.

It's a nice feeling. I allow myself to relax a little. After everyone has said hello, we funnel into the living room and take our seats.

The house is once again pristine, looking as though it never had dozens of people inside it over the weekend.

Mary has pulled in chairs from the dining room so that in addition to the couch and loveseats, there are still plenty of places to sit.

I take a seat at the end of the couch with Jenna on my left. Clara sits to her left, and the three of us engage in a bit of small talk about the weather. Mary emerges from the kitchen a few minutes later with a charcuterie board that looks so perfect it's like something straight out of a social media post.

The food plate is met with a chorus of *oohs* and *ahhs* as Mary sets it down on the coffee table. I can't help but marvel at it, too. Mary definitely knows how to host.

"I'll only be a few more minutes. Just need to pour the wine, and then we'll get started," Mary announces before stepping back out of the room.

Jenna pops up immediately.

"Let me help you," she says, stepping out after her.

Clara elbows me. "So, all moved in yet?"

"Finally, yes. Finished off the last of the boxes yesterday. Got a little shopping done earlier today, including this." I tap the cover of the book. "So we are officially moved in."

Clara claps her hands together. "Ooh, that's just so exciting! Aren't you just loving it here so far?"

I lick my lips, hesitating a second. Not sure if I'd use the word *loving* just yet, but I don't want to sour the mood, so I simply nod.

"Definitely still settling in, finding our rhythm," I say with a little smile.

Clara nods. "Oh, absolutely. It's a big change of pace out here, isn't it?"

That's true enough.

While it felt like there was always some minor catastrophe happening in the city, some loud siren or shout from outside, it's the polar opposite here. I think I still haven't gotten used to all the quiet, and maybe that's why Noah and I are so jumpy whenever we hear anything outside.

The book club meeting begins. I stay quiet for the first few minutes of it while Mary leads, asking us questions about the book and what we expect might happen next. After a little while, I feel comfortable enough to respond and do next time Mary asks a question.

Apparently she likes my answer, because she gives me a smile and a nod when I finish speaking. I take a sip of my wine happily. Seems like we're getting along just fine again.

Boosted by that success, I soon find myself engaging comfortably with the rest of the women, all of us sharing and laughing with each other.

I learn that just about everyone else here moved from the city too, during the past five years or so. The NYC exodus that seems all-too-common when people reach their thirties.

Clara actually has a pretty good sense of humor, continually making the group laugh. She tells one joke that has me doubled-over giggling, though that may just be the wine.

I've already had two glasses, because I didn't think

it'd be a good idea to refuse Mary's hospitality, not when things seem to be turning around for me.

By the time book club wraps up, I feel elated at how things have changed. I can't wait to get back and tell Noah that we might actually fit in here, after all. These people aren't so bad.

Maybe a little odd at times, but they're just people like us.

Mary shuts her book. "Okay, I think that about does it. See you all next week, same time."

I start to stand up, when Mary speaks to me specifically.

"And thank you Nikki for coming. I really enjoyed your contributions," she says with a smile.

I'm blushing a little as I thank her and say goodnight. Jenna gives my arm a squeeze as we follow the others, funneling out of the living room and into the main hallway.

"See? I knew everything would work out," she says then adds, "Also, before I forget—Mark and I would love to have you for dinner this week."

I nod, my cheeks slightly warm from the wine. "That sounds great. Tomorrow, I think Noah's working later, but Friday could work."

"Friday it is," she says.

She pulls me into another hug. She's pretty big on hugs, I'm starting to gather.

"I'm just so glad you're here. We're going to be such good friends. I can already tell. Like sisters," she says.

"I'm glad to be here," I reply.

It's actually true. Growing up, I always felt a little different from everyone else. I wasn't always into what was popular, and that sometimes had me feeling a little lonely and left out. Moving here is our chance to start over, a chance to reinvent ourselves.

Mary takes a few steps into the hallway from the kitchen side, waving goodbye to her guests.

Everyone in the foyer begins to hug and say goodbye. I make my way back to Mary. Again, maybe it's the alcohol, but I feel like we really made some progress today.

"Thanks again for inviting me," I say as I come to a stop in front of her.

Mary smiles. "Of course. You're one of us now."

I nod. "Really, I'm just very glad. And I hope that macaroni salad I made doesn't taste *too* terrible. I really don't have that much experience cooking."

Oh, look at me. Just babbling now. This is why I hardly drink.

"It's the thought that counts, so I wouldn't worry," Mary says with a chuckle.

We really do seem to have buried the hatchet. I'm more than relieved.

"I'm just glad we can move past my little snafu from the other day," I say, gesturing with my hands.

One of which flails to the side collides with something on the hallway table beside me.

I feel the cool surface of it on the back of my left hand for just a moment, and then I'm left to watch in horror as one of Mary's porcelain dolls sails through the air and smashes on the hard tile.

The entire house falls silent as the pieces scatter around our feet.

Oh no.

SIXTEEN

NIKKI

Shards of porcelain are absolutely everywhere.

My entire body is frozen in place. I can't stop staring at the floor, at the carnage of Mary's beloved doll.

I cannot believe that just happened. My eyes flick up to Mary, who stands there blinking as her brain works to register what just happened.

Then her cheeks flood with color.

"Mary—Mary I am so, so, sorry," I say, the words pouring out of me.

I reach for her arm, trying to make her understand that it was an accident, that I'm clumsy because I'm just a little tipsy.

Mary jerks away from me like I'm a toxic substance.

She licks her lips, and then her eyes flick up to the hallway again. There's no more warmth there.

"Book club is over. Goodnight," she says, her tone hard and unforgiving.

No one else has spoken, all of the other women

having stood stock-still since the doll broke. They probably didn't want to be guilty by association.

At Mary's words of dismissal, they begin to stream outside at record pace, silently pulling on rain jackets as they get to the door.

"Mary, please forgive me," I plead, again reaching out.

She turns up her nose and pulls away again.

"Thank you for coming, but I'm tired. I'd like you to leave now," she says.

My heart whirs in my chest. The night can't end like this. Not when things were going so well and starting to turn around for me.

"Mary, it was a complete accident. I'll—let me buy you a replacement," I say.

The house has mostly emptied of guests now. Only a couple other women beside me remain, and they're practically tearing holes in their jackets, they're putting them on so fast.

Lines form around Mary's mouth as it tightens into a smile devoid of all humor or happiness.

"The reason I treasured those dolls was for their rarity, which means replacing it will be nearly impossible. But it's fine."

The way she says *fine*, I know it's anything but.

"Mary, I—"

"I'm not angry, Nikki, just disappointed. Goodnight," Mary says.

My mouth clamps shut. Her emphatic tone makes it clear Mary doesn't want to hear anything else from me tonight.

I head for the door with my cheeks burning, pausing when I reach the doorway to look back at Mary once more. Her face still displays that tight-mouthed smile as our eyes meet.

It isn't a friendly one. Not at all.

"I'm sure I'll see you around," she says as she lowers herself to begin scooping up the pieces.

I drag the door shut and scamper down the steps like a dog with its tail between its legs. On the driveway I pause once more, wanting to walk back in there and apologize all over again or at least help her clean up.

But no, I shouldn't. Mary most definitely doesn't want to talk to me, not tonight. I want to slap myself.

How could I be so clumsy?

Everything had been forgiven. It was all going so well, and then I had to go and do something like that. Any residual buzz from the alcohol feels like it's burned off in the heat of my total embarrassment.

It happened in front of everyone, too. What a nightmare.

I'm ready to break down and cry, but I manage to hold it together while walking down the driveway. The other women are making their way to their homes up and down the street in both directions, though when I look up at them everyone hurriedly turns away from me.

I can't believe that just happened. Like, the worst possible outcome I could have even imagined, and somehow, I brought it to fruition.

The downstairs of our house is dark when I come back, Noah having already headed upstairs to start getting ready for bed. I find him in the bathroom, brushing his teeth.

When I push open the door, he turns to me with a foamy smile.

"Oh hey, how'd it—hey, what's wrong?"

I mean to tell him what happened, but as soon as I see his kind eyes, I burst into tears. The smile drops off Noah's face in an instant. He quickly spits into the sink then steps forward and pulls me into a hug.

I sob into his bare chest as I relate my big screw up. How everything is ruined now because of me.

Noah strokes my hair. I feel his neck move as he shakes his head above me, his chin grazing the top of my head.

"I'm sure it's not that bad. It was a mistake, that's all. Of course you wouldn't do that on purpose. I'm sure Mary can understand that."

His tone is so gentle, it makes me cry even more. I sniffle and reach for a tissue. Noah releases his hold on me so I can blow.

"You didn't see her face," I say. "She was not happy. I mean, she was pissed, Noah. You remember what Ron said when we first got to their house for the block party? He said it's like Mary loves those dolls more than him."

Noah nods silently. He remembers, and he knows I'm right.

My husband reaches up to scratch the back of his head like he always does when he's not sure what to say. I can tell he's trying to come up with something positive and encouraging, but nothing's coming.

"Maybe we can buy her another to make up for it," he finally suggests.

I shake my head. "Tried that. Apparently those dolls are super rare, or something."

"But maybe, right?" Noah says, meeting my eyes. "Like on Ebay or something?"

"Yeah. Maybe we can find one," I say, just so he doesn't worry about me anymore.

He's got to get to bed or he'll be wiped out at work tomorrow, and he shouldn't have to carry the burden of my screw-up. What's he going to do about it late at night anyway?

Noah pulls me into another hug, giving me a tight squeeze.

"We'll make this right. It's going to be okay."

Though I don't see how, I nod anyway, my chin moving up and down against his chest hair before Noah pulls away.

"You okay?"

"Yeah, I feel better," I lie before stepping out of the bathroom so he can finish up his nightly routine.

Out in the hallway, I rub the last of the tears from my eyes so he doesn't worry. The sink turns on again as Noah rinses his mouth and washes his face, while I do my best to pull myself together.

I know there's no chance I'm just going to just drift right off tonight, so I don't even try to shut my eyes once we lie down in bed.

Noah rolls over to my side to give me another kiss and double-checks that I'm alright before applying his mouth tape and turning over.

It doesn't take long for him to fall asleep, leaving me alone to torture myself with my thoughts to the soundtrack of his breathing.

I just can't believe myself. Those few terrible seconds keep replaying in my mind on a loop.

My sloppy hand gesture, my arm moving out just a few inches too wide. Connecting with the doll, registering the contact with just enough time to panic, but not enough time to do something to stop it.

The shrill crack of the doll as it split into dozens of tiny pieces on the tile. The absolute silence of the hallway in the seconds afterwards.

My cheeks begin to burn all over again, my body reacting to my rehashing of the event as if it's happening now.

Everything was going so well, too.

My stomach does a sickening flip as I think of Mary's humorless smile. That coldness in her voice as she wished me goodnight. She probably hates me now.

Noah thinks we can make this right, but I just don't know. He hasn't spent as much time around her as I have —plus he's a guy.

He messes up with one of his friends, and a six pack usually solves things. With Mary, I don't think it's going to be quite that simple.

The tightness in my gut makes me almost nauseous. I don't think I've been this consumed with anxiety since the night before my first day of high school.

I just can't stop thinking about what's going to come next.

When we first came here, everyone welcomed us

with open arms. Our new neighbors made every effort to bring us into the fold.

But if I've screwed that up here in the first few days, repaying insult for welcome, then what?

My mind drifts back to the two rings in the backyard. To the couple that lived here before us.

What if the group doesn't want us anymore after what I've done?

If we aren't a part of the group, where does that leave us?

SEVENTEEN

NIKKI

Waking up the next morning, I'm already filled with worry before my eyes are fully open.

People always say, "things will look brighter in the morning," when something bad happens, but that's not true in this case. They still look pretty bleak in the light of day.

Instead of waking to the sound of lawn mowers this morning, it's the squeal of the trash truck's brakes I hear as it comes to a stop either at our house or one nearby.

Noah's already gone, which means the house is empty once again. Another day of solitude.

That's starting to wear on me a little, if I'm being honest. Sure, it's nice having all this space, but there's something about being alone in a big house for hours on end that starts to mess with you. Especially when you're new to it all.

Back in New York City, being alone in an apartment no larger than a closet wasn't really a big deal. The city itself *is* your home. You hear the sounds of other lives pretty much twenty-four-seven, and if you want to see other people, you just step out your building's front door.

This is a different story.

I'm jumpier here. Every creak and bump has me on edge. It doesn't help that we've got another stormy day today, with the wind gusting and warm rain already beating down on the roof.

Peering out the kitchen windows reveals little besides a wall of rain as it overflows from the gutter above.

"Sorry, fella, looks like no outdoor fun times this morning," I say to Petey, who starts wagging his tail excitedly.

Oh, to be a dog. I scoop him up and pull open the back door, slipping my feet into Noah's hiking boots before clomping outside.

I can't let Petey out to do his business alone—not until I know what kind of wildlife might be prowling around out here. At his size he'd be no more than a mouthful for a coyote, and a hawk would no doubt see him as the perfect appetizer.

That means my dog needs a potty escort, rain or shine. I make a beeline for the grassy spot currently covered by the patio umbrella's overhang.

It only takes me a couple strides, but I'm nearly soaked to the bone by the time I set Petey down. He does a doggy shake, flinging droplets of water in every direction and dousing the few parts of me that managed to stay dry on the way here.

For a moment I worry that he's about to dash off into the yard, but wisely he thinks better of it and stays under the umbrella, trotting around in a slow circle as he looks for a spot to relieve himself.

At least it's warm out here, despite the downpour.

Once he's done, I scoop Petey back up and together we brave the wet dash to the back door.

Just before I step back inside, my vision catches on several puddles in the mulch beside the back door. The puddles are oblong, shaped almost like footprints. They line the entirety of the flowerbed. A shudder goes through my body.

Back inside, Petey gives another shake while I do something similar, shivering a little now that I'm inside the cool house and soaking wet. The open door lets in the sound of the drumming rain against the patio tiles.

It's a nice sound, but there's water leaking into the kitchen, so I pull the door shut.

After changing into dry clothes, I make some breakfast and eat at the small table in the kitchen while watching the downpour through the windows. At my feet, Petey busies himself with further decimating his roadkill toy.

Today is really the first day there isn't something that absolutely needs to get done around here.

A check of my phone shows me it's just after nine-thirty. It buzzes in my grip as Dad responds to my text from yesterday, saying the pictures of the house look great and he can't wait to see it in person. I send him back a heart emoji and then text that I miss him.

I'm missing everyone right now, actually. Noah, Emma, and all my other friends and acquaintances in the city. If I was ever feeling lonely in Manhattan, there was always someone I could text and hang out with.

Not quite the same deal here—and maybe it never will be, after last night's debacle.

I rub my face with my hand, feeling that twist of guilt in my stomach all over again. That look from Mary... yikes.

If it's true that she's sort of the ringleader of the group, what if she tells the other women not to see me?

We're supposed to go next door to Jenna and Mark's for dinner tomorrow. Hopefully that's still on the table after what I've done.

I pick up my phone again and do a search online for Mary's doll. I can see the little porcelain face clearly in my mind—I'll probably never forget it—and because it's burned into my brain, it's easy to determine there isn't anything like it immediately available.

Why couldn't I have just broken some two-dollar ceramic plate from a big box store?

I turn off my phone with a sigh and sit back in my chair. It probably isn't going to be good for me to sit around inside the house alone all day, moping about what happened. But where can I go?

There isn't really much of a town to speak of, save for a couple strip malls and big box stores. I'd have to order a ride to go somewhere anyway. With the rain coming down like it is, exploring the area doesn't seem all that appealing, either.

As I get up to put away my plate, I hear some sort of sound outside the front door. It pulls my attention up from my plate. Petey looks up with interest as well.

He isn't losing his mind barking, which tells me it might've been a delivery guy dropping off a package.

I dump the plate and utensils into the sink then head down the hallway to the front door. I peer through the foggy glass panels on the side of the door as I come up on it, but don't see any delivery van parked on the street. The door clicks as I unlock it.

Upon pulling it open, I look around but don't see anyone immediately in my field of vision. What I do see, however, is the yellow sheet of paper flapping in the wind beneath a rock on the doorstep.

Looking around again, I bend down to pick it up, sticking out a leg to block Petey from making a run for it.

The paper is folded and doesn't have any sort of marking on the outside. Once I unfold it, I just stand there a minute, staring at the printed words.

It's a notification of a fine for leaving our bins out on the curb past ten AM. Fifty dollars. I look up at the trash cans in disarray at the end of the driveway.

Then I check my phone. As I hold it up, I watch in real time as the digital clock display switches over to 10:01.

You can't be serious.

My cheeks flush with heat. Less than a minute after ten, and we've already been fined. Never mind the fact that it's pouring rain out there.

I reread the note, and then it hits me. I understand exactly what's going on here.

This is Mary's doing—she's head of the homeowners association.

It's revenge.

EIGHTEEN

NIKKI

I knew she was mad about the doll. I just knew it.

Now I've pissed off the head of our neighborhood's HOA within our very first week of moving here. Fantastic.

Drops of rain are starting to wet my socks, so with a final look around outside again, I push the door shut. The paper crumples slightly in my grasp as I stalk back into the kitchen and toss it onto the counter before pulling on Noah's hiking boots again.

What else can I do?

I'm sure at some point when we signed all those papers during the mortgage closing, we also signed something that said we agreed to follow every nitpicky little rule and regulation set forth by the HOA.

Now Mary's using that against me.

Grabbing my raincoat from the coat stand inside the door, I throw it over me and pull the door open again. I clop down the driveway in the oversized boots, shoulders hunched against the rain as it pummels down.

Mary must've been watching our house like a hawk, biding her time while the minutes ticked by.

I see that cold smile of hers in my mind as I grab the handle of the first garbage can. I'll bet she's probably watching now too, getting a real kick out of this.

A grunt escapes my lips as I hoist the second can upright and then teeter with them both back up the length of the driveway to put them on the side of the house.

Once that's done and I'm finally back inside and shaking off the rain, I head into the kitchen where the yellow sheet lies on the countertop. I smooth it back out and read over the print that informs me about how I'm supposed to pay the fine.

I take a picture of it and send it to Noah. He responds with a question mark, and I explain that we were a minute late taking in the trash cans. Then I text him that it's because of Mary.

He doesn't respond immediately, which makes my stomach twist. He's not mad at me, is he?

He *is* at work right now, after all, and probably busy. I'm just feeling guilty and putting thoughts into his head. Plus, I sort of feel like I let him down.

We're supposed to be a team here, working hard to make sure we do our part and acclimate to our new surroundings. Now I've gone and earned us a fifty-dollar fine. I feel irritated and guilty at the same time.

Folding the notification, I stuff it into my pocket for later. Not the best start to the day, that's for sure.

Petey wags his tail at my feet and nudges my leg with his cold little nose, always able to read how I'm feeling.

Right now? Not all that great.

Letting out a sigh as I plop down onto the couch, I fumble around the cushions for the remote. I've got a slight hangover from the wine last night, too.

A final parting gift for my stupidity. I check my phone again but no one's texted me. It's just me and Petey in this big house.

I throw on a movie but hardly pay any attention. I just can't stop thinking about how malicious the fine was. Mere seconds after the clock hit ten AM, and Mary was there to deliver the notification.

Clearly, she'd been planning this.

That makes my stomach tighten. I realize that I truly don't know this woman or what she's capable of. How long did she spend plotting her revenge against me?

The idea of her sitting there at her kitchen table with her husband, the two of them conspiring against me directly makes me very uncomfortable.

An hour or so passes with me paying very little attention to the story playing out on the TV screen in front of me. The next time I look outside, I see the rain has lessened to little more than a drizzle. A few drops drip down in front of the window from the edge of the gutter.

Something makes a bumping sound in the kitchen, making me sit upright with my throat tightening.

That's it. I can't just sit inside all day by myself.

"Time for a walk," I announce to Petey.

He couldn't be happier at the news, streaking to the door where he prances in eagerness while I retrieve my rain jacket and his leash.

Pulling on my own boots this time, I hook the chain to

Petey's collar and then we're out the door. I've got a small umbrella in hand just in case, but it doesn't look like I'll need it.

The sky is still gray, but there's no pressure there. The rain has come and gone. With Petey leading the charge, we make our way to the street.

I just want to walk around some to clear my head. A little exercise should do me good. Plus, a part of me wants to walk by Mary's house, too. Show her this little game she's playing isn't going to beat me.

We take a right at the end of the driveway and start around the circle. Petey's tugging to get closer to the circle of trees in the center. Probably a haven for all the squirrels and other little animals to hang out in. I oblige him, and together we drift across the street until we're at the little white fence that encircles the copse of trees.

Petey's still pulling hard, and I take a few steps up onto the wet grass to accommodate his mission. He must have picked up the scent of squirrel. Maybe a dead bird.

That thought makes me pull back a little, as I'm not too sure I want to see a bird carcass right now. I'm already not feeling great, and some poor dead bird might just do me in.

Petey refuses to give in, though. We're just a couple steps from the edge of the miniature forest, which is surrounded by a border of grass almost like a moat before it transforms into pine-needle-covered dirt inside.

I'm warily checking that pine-needled dirt in a half-squint in case there really is a deceased animal when I spot something stuck there in the mud. Just off to our right, at the base of one of the evergreen trees.

I take another step forward. What is that?

Petey tugs at the leash, moving toward it with interest, his tail wagging.

The ground here is very waterlogged, and it squelches beneath my steps as I reach down into the muck and pick up the mystery object.

It takes a moment to pull it up, the mud seeming to fight against me before releasing the thing with a wet sucking noise.

It's plastic... a blank face mask.

That on its own is strange, given we're nowhere near Halloween, but that isn't what has me worried.

It's the two droplets of what I think is *blood* that dot the top of it.

NINETEEN

NIKKI

I stare hard at the drops.

That is blood, isn't it?

Holding it up now, I just don't know for sure. It's a dark-reddish hue, but so is the mud. Looking at the muddy spot beneath the tree where I found the mask doesn't reveal any clues. If there were any, the rain probably washed them away.

The mask itself is pretty terrifying. It's made from completely blank, slightly opaque plastic that blurs my hand to the point I can only make out my skin tone beneath it. On a face, it might erase features altogether.

I swallow and look up, suddenly aware I'm plainly visible to everyone around me.

Someone was wearing this, for whatever reason. I glance at the houses across from me, my heart thudding heavily in my chest as I clutch tight to the mask.

I'm not sure what to do. Do I call the police? Call Noah?

I'm still not even sure that there's actually blood on

the edge of it. Not to mention if it is, there's literally only two drops. Is that enough to get them to send a cruiser out here?

Looking back up the street, I suddenly remember something. Lily is a nurse, and she lives right up the road. She'll be able to tell if this is blood or not.

And if it isn't, maybe she'll be able to tell me why this creepy mask might be sitting out here in the middle of summer. For some reason, I feel like I can talk to her about it.

Maybe it's because out of everyone at that block party, she was the only person who didn't seem like they were... acting in some way.

Everyone else was all small talk and big smiles.

I start walking across the grass and then reach the pavement again, Petey trotting along beside me as we head up the street. As I go, I swear I can feel someone watching me.

Turning around, my eyes are pulled to movement in a window at the very back of the cul-de-sac. A curtain drops as I stand there.

My heart thuds. Someone *was* watching me. I look around again but don't see any more movement on the street. In fact, it's completely, totally silent.

I don't hear a car, a voice, anything.

Just the gentle brush of the breeze as it sweeps a warm gust of air over me. Readjusting my grip on Petey's leash, I continue up the road.

Coming out of the circle of the cul-de-sac, the road is still silent on either side. Driveways sit empty like I'm standing in a ghost town. Everyone's already gone to work. Hopefully Lily is home and isn't working a shift right now.

At the block party, I heard it mentioned that her house was the gray one with white shutters. It sits just as quiet as all the rest, windows still shiny from the downpour as I approach.

The curtains are pulled shut, too.

"Come on Pete," I say, urging him up the long driveway.

He's got his little head turned around as he peers behind us, as if there's something or someone there. But when I glance back, I don't see anything. It's still deathly quiet, too.

After another second, I manage to convince him to get his little legs moving again, and we continue up Lily's driveway. A small silver wind spinner in the flowerbed draws my attention with its pattern that seems to fold in on itself as it spins.

The garage door is closed, but I can see through the windows and confirm there is a car in there, so hopefully Lily is home. I arrive at the doorstep. After another look down at Petey, I knock.

For almost thirty seconds I don't hear anything, but then there's the sound of footsteps from inside. I hear a lock click—and then another.

And another.

And another.

Finally the door opens a crack, and Lily's bright blue eye fills the gap.

"Yeah? What do you want?" she asks.

"I..." I start, still a little taken aback by what had to be the sound of at least four locks unlocking.

Slowly I lift up the mask in my hand.

"I found this, and—"

Lily's eyes go wide, and then the door swings open. She's wearing a cropped tee with the logo of a band I love, but what catches my attention is the knife she's got clutched in her grasp.

"What..."

"What do you mean, you found that?" Lily says quickly, interrupting me.

"It was in the mud, by that little wooded area in the cul-de-sac," I say, feeling bewildered.

Lily's eyes flick back and forth wildly in a scan of the street before she snakes out a hand and grabs the front of my coat. I let out a yelp of surprise as she pulls me inside and shuts the door again.

"What's going on? Why are you holding a knife?" I ask, my eyes following her as she steps over to the window and peers out between the curtains. I cast a glance around the room, taking it all in.

She doesn't respond, choosing instead to watch the outdoors for a few more seconds. Petey sniffs at the interior of the unfamiliar house with interest.

"Lily," I say.

This time, she looks over at me.

"What?"

"Why do you have that knife? What's going on?" I ask. My heart is beating furiously in my chest.

Lily looks down at the blade in her hand, as if she

didn't realize she was even holding it. She places it down on the windowsill in front of her.

"You really haven't gotten it yet?" she asks.

"Gotten what?"

Lily licks her lips and then gestures around us. "This place. This neighborhood. It isn't a normal neighborhood."

My eyebrows furrow, and my stomach takes a big roller-coaster dive. "What do you mean?"

She jerks a thumb at the window, behind her now that she's turned to face me. "Haven't you noticed something weird about everyone here, how they all act the same?"

"Like you were saying at the block party," I say, swallowing.

I'm just relieved to hear that someone else has noticed something strange going on around here, too. It's not just me, and it's not just me being the new girl.

"It's almost like a clique in high school or something, or a college sorority," Lily says.

I point at the windowsill. "That still doesn't explain the knife."

Lily chews her lip, looking as if she's debating telling me something.

"What?" I ask.

My heart thuds in my chest. I need to know what is going on around here, and what kind of situation Noah and I have unwittingly moved into. I raise up the mask.

"What does *this* have to do with everything? Why were you so freaked out when you saw it?"

"Because that's what they wear," Lily says, the words bursting out of her suddenly.

I blink. "Who wears?"

Lily shakes her head. "I don't... I don't know exactly—hence the masks. It's like there's this secret club here, some special in-group that you only really know of if you're in it."

I cross my arms. "Then how do you know about it?"

Lily's eyes drop to the rug. "Because I saw that mask on the night my husband went missing."

TWENTY
NIKKI

Okay, pause.

What in the world is going on around here?

"Your husband is missing?" I ask.

At the party, she told me she'd lost her husband. I assumed something tragic like a car accident or cancer.

Lily nods. "It happened almost two years ago. We had just moved in here, like you. One night as I was leaving for work, I saw these two people standing on the street wearing masks just like that."

"That next morning, I got a call at the hospital saying my husband never showed up for work. And he hasn't been seen since," Lily finishes.

Wait a minute. I saw two people standing out on the street, too.

And now that I'm thinking back on it, it suddenly makes so much more sense as to why I had such a hard time deciphering their faces. It's not because my eyesight is starting to go, it's that they were wearing masks which made it impossible.

I nod, my throat suddenly dry. "I saw two people standing outside my house the other night. They just stood and stared at my house for like a minute straight."

My face feels flushed. If I were alone, all of this would sound crazy, but it's not just me thinking it. Lily is right here with me, nodding and agreeing.

"Sounds like exactly what I saw that night. When the police came and searched the house, the conclusion they drew was that he probably just got sick of being married and took off. Investigation ended there."

"But you think they might've had something to do with it," I say, biting my lip. "The people in the masks."

"I don't know," Lily says, throwing up her hands. "Could just be coincidence. And that's the whole point. They make you... they make you question everything. All the time. You get to a point where it's just... you don't know what to expect next."

"Hence the knife," Lily says, her arm coming up to point at it before dropping back down to her side.

"But I haven't seen the mask since—until you showed up just now," she says.

"But who are these people in the masks? And what do they want?" I ask, holding it up again.

Lily shakes her head. "I don't know. No one does unless they're in the club. Some of the people around here are, and some aren't. But I'll tell you what I *do* know. What everyone knows—whoever they are, you don't want to be on their bad side."

I swallow hard, thinking back on my disastrous first week here. Suddenly it hits me—I only saw the people in the masks *after* the macaroni salad incident.

"Bad side?" I ask weakly, my throat tightening.

"Trust me, it's horrific. Everything they can do to make your life a living nightmare, they'll do. Fines, ostracization, messing with your home, your car, your job—all of it."

Lily's voice trails off as she looks into the distance before clearing her throat.

"And the worst part is, it's never outright harassment, at least not anything that can be proven," she says. "That's why everyone around here dresses the same, acts the same. Everyone is terrified of bringing attention to themselves, of stepping out of line. Do what everyone else is doing, and maybe you can blend in and stay afloat."

My chest burns as I picture the yellow paper under the rock on my doorstep. *A living nightmare.*

"So it's Mary. She's involved in this secret club," I say, forcing the words out.

Lily nods. "It makes sense she's involved, but again, nothing can be proven. But it's pretty obvious if you're looking for it. What Mary says, goes. It's like the law around here."

And I've just pissed her off royally.

What Lily is describing, having your every aspect of your life turned upside down, has now begun happening to *me.*

"I got a fine," I blurt out.

"Just today. I got a sheet of paper saying I owe fifty dollars for not taking my trash bins in before ten. At 10:01."

Lily nods knowingly. "Consider that a warning. From

them. If you don't want to live in misery, I'd say try to blend in like everyone else."

My eyes dart back and forth as I attempt to digest all of this new—and totally bizarre—information.

I wish Noah was here with me right now, so I wouldn't have to try and explain all of this to him. I can see myself trying, panicky words gushing out of me in waves, leaving Noah confused and slightly worried.

A warning. A message from Mary to clean up my act and to fall in line.

If what Lily says is true, and this group-within-the-group really can ruin your life, maybe I should take her advice. Just pay my fine and tell Noah to start wearing more polo shirts like the rest of the husbands around here.

I blink and shake my head. What am I even saying? I've never been one to follow the crowd—not since I was a little girl trying to dye my hair purple by smashing black-berries into it. If there's one thing consistent about me, it's that I've never been one to go with the grain.

I look back up at Lily and then extend the mask out to her. "I want you to look at this and tell me if that's blood right there."

Lily's eyes drop to the mask and then whip back up to my face. "Blood?"

I nod, pointing at the two suspicious drops. She holds up a finger and then dashes into the kitchen, re-emerging moments later with a magnifying glass.

She takes the mask from me and carries it over to a lamp to hold it up to the light. As she does, I get another look at the mask as it would appear on a person. It's so horrifyingly blank, so devoid of everything that makes a human face human.

"Yeah... I think that is blood. Dried blood. Certainly looks like it," Lily says after another long moment of inspection.

"Then I want to call the police," I say immediately.

Lily's eyes dart over to me. "*What*? Didn't you hear a word I just said? You don't want to be on their bad side. Like *at all*."

"There's freaking *blood* on a creepy mask, Lily. The same kind of mask that the last time you saw it, your husband disappeared. How can we not call the police?" I ask.

"Because there's no crime. The police will just log it and forget it, like they always do. I'm telling you, all calling them is going to do is bring their wrath upon you," she says.

"How do we know there's no crime? Maybe that blood belongs to another missing person. We just don't know," I say, refusing to back down.

This is absolutely the kind of thing you're supposed to call the police about, right?

Honestly, my only experience with the cops besides speeding tickets is TV shows and movies. They're always scraping blood samples for DNA evidence, right? It's the kind of clue that leads to a case being blown wide open at the end of an episode.

Lily can tell I'm not going to change my mind about this and throws up her hands.

"Fine. We can call, but you'll see. And don't come

crying to me when everything starts to fall apart for you," she says.

I shake my head. "We still need to call. Someone needs to know about this."

Lily chews her lip. "Okay. But if the cops ask us to go outside and talk or something, I'm not going."

"Fine," I say.

Lily makes the call. It takes almost twenty minutes for a policeman to arrive, but finally I see the cruiser pull alongside the curb in front of Lily's house.

She's in the kitchen making tea while I watch through the window.

"He's here," I say over my shoulder.

Lily nods and comes back into the living room. The car door slamming shut gets Petey's attention, his little head popping up with interest.

It's started to drizzle again, dampening the top of the officer's head as he rounds the car. The man is big, burly, and looks to be all business as he walks up the driveway. The radio on his belt warbles and beeps as he walks.

I wipe my palms on the front of my jean shorts as Lily picks up the mask with a gloved hand again.

A knock at the door. Petey lets out a bark, bouncing excitedly around my feet as Lily and I walk toward the door. Before opening it, Lily looks at me again, and I nod.

"Mrs. Porter? I'm Officer Breckman, you called about a bloody mask," the officer says as Lily opens the door for him.

"Yes, we did," Lily says, holding it up.

Petey's yips are making it sort of hard to hear what she's saying.

"Actually my neighbor Nikki here found it, but she wasn't sure if that was actually blood on the top there. I'm a nurse, so she brought it to me. And it is blood—at least I'm pretty sure it is."

Officer Breckman inspects the mask in Lily's hand for a moment before his eyes slide to me.

"Nikki?" he asks in a voice loud enough to be heard over Petey.

I nod quickly. "Petey, hush—that's right."

"And your last name is?"

"Anderson. I just moved here."

Breckman nods curtly. "And you found this mask?"

"Yeah. In a wooded area down the street, in the center of the cul-de-sac," I say.

Officer Breckman peers down the road and then looks back at me. "Could you show me, please?"

"Absolutely," I say.

Petey's still excitedly barking, and I can tell Officer Breckman isn't super into all the loud noise. But at least he's still here and seems to be taking this seriously.

He didn't immediately burst into laughter, which was honestly one of my fears. That all of this is all some big joke being played by someone with a sick sense of humor.

My blood is pumping now. I'm not entirely sure about what I'm doing, but I continue, pulling on my rain-coat and stepping outside to lead Officer Breckman down the street.

"Can you watch Petey for just a minute?" I ask Lily.

She opens her mouth but then sighs and nods.

"Yeah. Okay. Fine." she says before pushing the door shut.

The two of us head down the driveway. I can hear the officer's radio make some noise, and he picks it up to reply in some police code. The light drizzle makes me pull my raincoat over my head as we go.

"When did you find the mask?" Officer Breckman asks me.

"About an hour ago. But I don't know how long it's been there, because I just moved in last week."

Breckman nods, but hasn't written down anything yet. My heart starts to sink. Does that mean he isn't taking this seriously after all?

Maybe he thinks I'm some bored housewife with nothing better to do than call the cops on my neighbors, just to spice up the day. I clear my throat, glancing at his face, trying to read his expression without obviously studying him. Breckman is like a brick wall—completely impassive.

Walking down the street with my rain boots squeaking, I cast a glance up at the other houses around us. Someone moves across a window in the house two down from mine.

I think of Lily's words again. *Like living in a nightmare.*

Well, it's too late to go back now. They've seen me with a police officer, which means word will spread all through the neighborhood. But I couldn't live with myself if I didn't call this in. Someone out there could be seriously hurt, or even dead.

Who knows? Maybe I can put a stop to all this craziness right now.

We reach the tree-filled area in the center of the cul-de-sac, and I lead Officer Breckman over to the spot where I found the mask.

"It was lying in the mud right there," I say, pointing to the spot at the base of the tree.

The cop walks over and squats down in the mud beside the spot, eyeing it a moment before reaching around his belt for a long, heavy flashlight that he flicks on and shines into the grime.

"Don't see any more blood," he says.

Flipping the flashlight around, he gently probes the mud with the butt of the thing to see if there's anything else buried in the area. Nothing comes up, and a few moments later he's getting back to his feet, knees popping.

"Okay, then. If you'd like, I can take the mask back to the station, see if we've come across something like it before." Breckman flicks mud off the end of the flashlight before sliding it back into his belt.

"That's it?" I ask, feeling my shoulders slump.

I'm not sure what I was expecting. Maybe for Breckman to go digging in the mud before scrambling for his radio, calling all units?

Lights, sirens. Doors getting busted down. Instead, the officer looks me over.

"As far as I can tell, no crime has been committed, Ma'am. Now if there was more blood, I'd say there might be something going on. But given it's a couple drops, I'd wager we're dealing with a nosebleed, maybe a cut lip."

Officer Breckman gestures behind him. "Some kid probably went running through the dark in the mask, bumped into a tree."

"But what about DNA sampling? Running some analysis? What if the person that bled is hurt, or missing?" I ask, exasperated.

Breckman eyes me and he adjusts the fit of his belt. "I'm sorry, Mrs. Anderson. But we're a small, small town here in Peerskill, which means an even smaller budget. If there was more evidence, I might be able to send the mask out somewhere, have it looked at, but there's not, so my hands are tied. I'm sorry."

I let out another breath. There's nothing else to say, really. Officer Breckman does have a point.

Maybe it really is just a nosebleed. If it were something more, wouldn't there be more blood?

It has rained quite a lot over the past couple days, though. That could've easily washed away any more evidence.

"I'll... I'll ask around the station, see if anyone else has heard of anything with masks in the area," Breckman adds.

I look up at him. "Thanks. I appreciate you coming out."

We start back up the road toward Lily's as Breckman radios in and gives more police-speak. And that's that.

It takes a couple minutes, but soon we're coming up on his police cruiser parked outside Lily's house again.

Only this time, the street is no longer empty. Five people stand huddled on the other side of the street and up a ways, watching and conversing among themselves as they try to figure out what's going on.

"I'll take your number, and let you know if there's any news," Breckman says as we reach his vehicle.

I see Lily peer out from between her curtains again as the policeman gets my information. Then he's loading up into his cruiser and pulling away from the curb.

There's nothing I can do but watch the red glow of his taillights as he reaches the end of the street and pauses at the stop sign before turning right. Rain continues to drizzle down, droplets falling in front of my eyes as I stand there.

Looks like Lily was right, and the police weren't much help. As I start back up her driveway, my eyes flick over to the five people standing and watching.

They're still there, but they're no longer talking.

Now, they're all staring at me.

The time until Noah gets home is spent mostly by the window, peering through the blinds at the street outside.

It's empty, as it has been basically all day. The rain slowed a couple hours ago, allowing the fading blue of the sky to peek through as the day wanes on. The asphalt is shiny with puddles that cast reflections of the clouds above.

It's almost seven, and Noah still isn't back. With each minute that passes without him pulling into the driveway, the thoughts in my head grow louder.

The thoughts about Lily's husband, and the call she received that he'd never showed up for work.

My stomach tightens even more. What if because of me, Noah won't be coming home at all?

And then I see headlights at the top of the cul-de-sac circle. It's Noah. He's here.

I stand, my face flushing with relief as I take a breath. My palms tingle as I smear them on my jean shorts and run a hand through my hair.

There's so much that Noah needs to hear about. I'm buzzing with adrenaline as he pulls into the driveway and turns off the car. A moment later I hear the car door open and shut, and then he's coming up the path to the door.

I can't wait that long and open it myself. Noah leans back in surprise, his keys in hand ready to unlock it.

"Well, hello Mrs—" he begins, but I cut him off.

"I need to tell you something. Right now," I say.

Noah's face changes immediately. "What's wrong?"

I pull him inside with another glance out at the street before shutting the door and locking it.

"Nikki, what's going on?" Noah asks.

There's a note of tension in his voice, no doubt at my odd demeanor.

Turning around, I take a deep breath. Then I fill him in on everything that happened today after receiving the fine. Finding the mask, the conversation with Lily, and finally what happened with Officer Breckman.

When I'm finished, Noah is silent for a few seconds as he works over everything I've told him.

"Okay," he says finally.

"So, what do we do? Call the police?"

"I just tried that, remember? This group, whoever they are, they're really careful. Lily says they never leave any trace of what they do—except for this mask, I guess."

Noah shakes his head. "Now I think I'm starting to realize why we were able to get such a good deal on this house."

A knock on the door behind me has both of us jumping.

"Who is that?" Noah hisses, crouching down out of instinct.

He's still holding his briefcase, only now he's wielding it like a weapon as he takes a step to the side to peer through the foggy panels of glass beside the door.

"Who is it?" I whisper, my heart up in my throat.

Is it *them*? Did they see me with the cop earlier and have come to teach me a lesson?

"It's one of the neighbors... Jenna, I think? Was that her name?"

Suddenly I remember we made plans for Noah and I to go over there for dinner. But that's tomorrow, not today.

"It's Jenna," I hear her call from outside.

Noah looks at me, and at my nod, reaches over and unlocks the door. We both peer through the tiny crack at her as she stands there wearing a light cardigan over a preppy summer dress.

"Hi there, she says, "I'm sorry to be the bearer of bad news, but it looks like tomorrow night won't work for us after all."

"Mark forgot to tell me about this party they're having for a coworker," she adds.

Right. I'm sure it has nothing to do with the fact that I —and Noah by extension—are now persona non grata around here.

Jenna doesn't want to be seen with us.

"Right," I say.

I keep my face blank, but I can tell Jenna knows I'm not buying it.

"Maybe next time," she says, the smile struggling just

a little bit before she says goodbye and walks off the doorstep.

We shut the door but continue to watch her through the foggy glass panels. Jenna is speed-walking away, as if she doesn't want to spend another second near our house.

So much for being *sisters*.

"Well, great, there goes Friday night. And to think I bought a nice bottle of wine to bring over," Noah says, chewing his lip.

He steps away from the door.

"I guess I can tell Emma she's good to come up earlier and spend the night," I say.

Noah nods as he peers through the blinds, his neck craning as he looks out.

"You think that was because of you calling the cops?"

I nod. "It's got to be, right? It's like Lily said—do something Mary doesn't like and face the consequences."

"But that was just a couple hours ago," Noah says.

"Secrets don't stay secrets long in the suburbs I guess."

He lets his arm drop down to his side. "Yeah."

I can tell he's disappointed by the turn of events and feel a pang of guilt in my chest at that. Noah and Mark seemed like they were really getting along at the block party, and I guess Noah was hoping that would turn into friendship.

After what I did though, I doubt Mark will be calling Noah up anytime soon.

Later on in the evening when I go upstairs to get ready for bed, I find Noah standing in the hallway, the dull glow of his phone illuminating his face.

"Huh," he says after another couple seconds.

"What?"

He shakes his head. "I just... I think the neighborhood guys just removed me from the group chat we made to watch the game this weekend. I don't see the texts anymore."

There's going to be a lot of that, I expect. Whatever goodwill we earned over the first couple of days here is long gone.

Sounds like Mary has just made a new rule: No Andersons.

By the time we climb into bed, we're both exhausted. Despite that, it takes me forever to fall asleep. Noah's breathing hasn't reached that usual even pace it usually does, which tells me he's on his side of the bed thinking over it all too.

I can't stop ruminating on everything I learned today. The secret club that seemingly rules the neighborhood, run by the one person I wasn't supposed to piss off.

Lily's warning to me.

Maybe I should've thought twice about calling the cops when Lily was literally too afraid to come outside with me to go inspect the spot where I found the mask. It's too late now.

I turn onto my side, my stomach in knots over what's going to come next. Mary knows about me calling the police. Given she was watching the house like a hawk this morning, I'm absolutely certain of it.

Jenna's dinner cancellation and Noah's group chat removal practically confirms that. Mary's already begun exacting her revenge, using her influence over the neighborhood.

We've officially been shunned.

The question now is... what comes next?

TWENTY-TWO
NIKKI

Once again, Noah's already left for work when I wake up.

He must've just left though, because I hear the car start up in the driveway and then roll down it. I sit up and rub my face, grabbing for my phone to check the time.

7:43 AM, much earlier than I usually get up.

I let out a yawn, somehow feeling even more exhausted than when I went to sleep last night. It was the worst night of sleep I've had yet.

At best, I'd say I got maybe three hours total. The rest of the time was spent with my eyes wide and heart pounding as I stared into the darkness wondering what's going to happen next.

Pushing off the covers, I take a few staggering steps across the carpet toward the bathroom door. Another huge yawn rips through me as I rub an eye and pull the door open.

Inside, I make my way to the toilet and plop down, my chin drooping a little as I sit there.

Then I hear lawnmowers—all at once. It's like one moment there was silence, and then the next the mowers began in some kind of landscaping chorus.

My head comes back up, the sleepiness gone as I flush and go to the bathroom window to look out. I can't see anyone mowing grass, but the distinctive noise is there now as it has been every time I've woken up later. I've just never been up this early to hear it start.

I glance down at my phone. 7:45, on the dot. Another of Mary's rules?

No mowers before then, no doubt. I blink a couple times as I try to work through another thought.

I've been enjoying the sound of distant mowers waking up every morning—seeing it as the suburb's version of city noise—but now that I think of it, it's quite literally *every* morning.

There are a fair number of people in the neighborhood, but every day?

Walking downstairs, I've already got a strange feeling, carried over from yesterday and amplified by the symphony of lawn sounds outside.

Petey's up, but he doesn't rush over to me when I come downstairs.

Instead, he's focused intently on the front door again. Instantly my pulse begins to quicken.

Is there someone there?

Noah's already left, which means it's just me here. But Petey isn't growling, he's just looking with interest. Like he did when Mary left the paper on the doorstep.

I creep to the door and look through the glass, catching sight of a flash of bright yellow on the top step.

Pulling open the door, I know exactly what it is. Under a stone is another folded sheet of paper. Once again I scan the street, but it's empty. I pick up the paper with my heart thudding against my ribcage.

Shutting the door, I hastily unfold the notification.

Another fine. This one is eighty-five dollars. *For grass below 1 inch, or above 1.5 inches*, it reads.

Well, that explains the mowers. I crumple the sheet of paper and throw it into the living room, feeling my blood boil. I bet if I went out there right now, I'd measure the grass at something like 1.51 inches.

Mary's toying with me. Trying to punish me for breaking her doll, for telling the police about the mask. I peer through the window up the street, where I can just make out the corner of Lily's house up the road.

It looks quiet as usual. Hopefully she's doing okay up there. I let out a sigh and turn around to make myself some breakfast when I freeze, my gaze riveted on the back patio through the open window blinds.

Then I'm stalking over to the back door and yanking it open in a rush. Petey shoots out before I can stop him but freezes when I shout his name.

"Petey, no! Watch out. There's glass everywhere," I say.

Thinking he's in trouble, the little dog scurries back toward me with his tiny tail tucked between his legs. I scoop him up and kiss him so he knows he didn't do anything wrong as I observe the wreck of our patio.

The glass coffee table is completely shattered, nuggets of the safety-glass tabletop absolutely everywhere. There's a gnarled wood branch balanced against the metal frame, as if that was the culprit.

A glance up at the trees along the side of the house shows a light colored-spot where the branch broke off.

After what Lily said, however, I know better.

This was *them*.

And just like she said, there's no way to prove it.

It rained and stormed for hours yesterday, and the wind continued into the night. From an outside perspective, a branch could've easily been weakened and finally given way during the night.

That's exactly what they want it to look like, too.

I chew my lip and rub Petey's soft belly again as I look over the scene. It'll take hours to pick up every little piece of glass from between the patio tiles. It looks like some of them even made their way onto the grass.

Petey definitely won't be allowed to run out here for a while. I pull out my phone and take a picture for documentation and to show Noah.

He replies with an angry-faced emoji within minutes.

Back inside, I manage to swallow a couple bites of scrambled eggs, though I don't have much of an appetite. Emma's supposed to be here in a few hours, and she can't come soon enough.

It's clear Mary's punishment didn't end with Jenna's cancellation and a couple of petty fines. Now they're destroying our property. If that actually was Mary's doing, and not just the weather.

It had to be her, right?

It's maddening, and I'll bet that's probably the point.

Leaving a person wondering, never certain of anything until... until what?

I don't know what the endgame is here. Until we move out? My heart pangs.

Or until our rings end up like the pair we found in the backyard?

I swallow hard and peer through the blinds at the outside world. It's a wonderfully sunny day, the complete opposite of yesterday, and yet I have zero interest in being out there.

There's movement visible between the branches of the trees in the cul-de-sac. People are walking around the curve, coming this way. I duck down, though there's no chance that I could've been spotted.

It's Jenna and another woman I recognize from the block party whose name I've forgotten.

The two of them are decked out in their bright workout outfits. Jenna's is hot pink, the spandex tights swishing back and forth as she walks swiftly with the other woman.

I can't help but watch them as they make their way up the street.

Jenna is absolutely a follower, keenly intent on fitting in and getting along. I think I knew that much from the moment I first met her. Her cancelling our dinner plans furthers the point.

This begs the question as to whether she did it out of fear, or because she's one of them. I truly don't know.

I wish there was a way to figure this out without alerting the rest of the neighborhood.

If I were to pull her aside and try to talk with her

about any of this, I'm absolutely certain word would make its way back to Mary within hours.

There are just too many windows, too many watchers.

If we're going to get through this thing, we need to know who's on our side and who's not. I know Mary has her clique, which means maybe we need to try and start our own.

I chew my lip as Jenna and the other woman walk up the street directly in front of our house. My heart beats a little faster as I see their heads turn, gazing at our house for just a second before picking up their pace and moving on.

They're talking about us. Right now, as they exercise.

It's probably all anyone can talk about around here. I think again of the small group that stood by silently as I spoke with Officer Breckman.

Amid a few blank faces, I saw some worry, too.

Worry that I was upsetting the order of things around here, or worry for me?

Who knows? There's no chance I'll be able to ask anyone, either. I think if I try to approach anyone, they might actually run away from me like I've got cooties or something.

Only a few more hours until Emma arrives. I need interaction. I need a friend. Now that I know I won't be making any around here, Emma's being here means even more to me.

Besides Jenna and her friend earlier, I don't see anyone else outside the rest of the day, but that doesn't stop me from checking the windows every few minutes.

It's almost impossible to focus on anything, as my brain keeps returning to my conversation with Lily yesterday.

All I want right now is for someone to be with me so that I'm not so alone all the time.

Noah's still at work and will be for the next several hours. Back in the city, we never got to have all that much time together, given he works in-person, but now with the extra commuting time tacked on top, there's even less time than before.

The more days that pass, the more I'm starting to regret moving at all. On paper, it sounds wonderful. All that space. A yard. New friends and neighbors.

No one mentions what happens when you don't fit into the mold of the established order.

While Noah's affected by this too, it's not as much as I am. He's got a job to go to, a way to get out of here for a few hours each day. Not me.

We're lucky enough that with Noah's recent promotion, I was able to quit my bartending job. At first I was elated, because that meant I finally had some time to start writing songs again. Now, sitting here with nowhere to go, nothing to do but stare outside and worry?

Not so much.

Fear and anxiety isn't really conducive to creativity. At least Emma's coming tonight. I just need to occupy myself until then.

The day passes with me half-watching some daytime TV while on my phone, looking up HOAs. I come across a few forums where people are griping about how strict and unforgiving theirs is.

If only they knew what we're going through over here. They'd count themselves lucky.

After turning off the TV, I'm once again left to sit in silence. It really is isolating, being out here alone.

I think about walking up to see Lily but think better of it. She's probably working a shift right now, anyway.

The hours seem to drift by in a haze, until eventually the afternoon is finished and becomes the evening.

Finally I hear the sound of a car pulling up in front of the house and leap to my feet.

A car door opens and shuts. Emma. She's here.

She thanks the ride service driver, and the car pulls off. I rush to the door and pull it open.

When she sees me, Emma shrieks and rushes forward.

We hug, exclaiming about how much we missed each other while squeezing tight.

"Ugh, I know it's only been like a week, but it feels like a year! How are you?" she asks as we pull apart.

I grimace. I've never been able to keep things from her, so after cracking open the expensive bottle of wine meant for Jenna and Mark, I tell her everything, every bizarre detail.

"See this is why I'm never leaving the city," Emma says with a nod.

She takes another sip from her wine glass before craning her neck to peer out through the back windows at the patio.

"It's crazy in New York, sure. But I know that kind of crazy. It's this bored, suburban crazy that really scares me," she says.

"You might be right about that," I say with a hard nod.

"And there's nothing you can do? You just have to pay these fines?" Emma asks.

"I guess it's the rule. HOA decides something, that's the end of the conversation," I say.

"That sucks worse than a broken vacuum," Emma says angrily, taking another swig.

"I'm pissed for you, Ki."

I pour myself another glass from the bottle. My cheeks feel a little warm from the alcohol. This isn't anything like being at the block party, though, and I'm not worried about having a little too much to drink.

I'm safe here with Emma, my best friend.

"And this... Mary, she's the one who's doing all this?" Emma asks.

"Yeah. She's like the head cheerleader, I guess."

"So *she's* the one I've got to kill," Emma says, nodding with a straight face.

That makes me giggle. "That's sweet of you, Em. Thanks."

She pats my hand. "Of course. It'd be my pleasure."

We lean back on the couch and stare up at the ceiling, our wine glasses in hand. Any minute now, Noah should be getting home. Then I'll have all my people here, at least for the weekend.

I can't keep dealing with this all by myself.

While it's nice to call and text with Emma, having her here in person with me is just a whole different experience. It's like everything will be okay, despite the craziness. I no longer feel so alone.

After she leaves though, it'll be back to business as usual, and I'm dreading it even though she just got here.

I take another long sip of my wine, letting it swirl around my mouth before swallowing.

"So given everything you've told me, this suddenly puts things into perspective, but Max and I broke up," Emma blurts out.

My head whips over to her. "What? When?"

She nods. "Last night. I figured I'd wait until I got here to tell you, because trying to talk about it over the phone just wouldn't do."

I'm already pushing off the couch. "We're going to need another bottle of wine."

"Come on, the wine fridge is downstairs. I'll show you the basement."

Emma stands up too, though she wobbles just a bit, steadying herself on the couch arm. We head downstairs as Emma begins telling me how the breakup went down. I flip the light switch and we head down the basement stairs.

The basement is semi-finished, with a main room that Noah's started to turn into a home gym and a second room for storage. We reach the tiled floor and head toward the wine cooler, which is on the opposite wall.

"I can't believe him," I say over my shoulder as I pull open the door of the small storage fridge on the floor.

Emma nods. "And it was his *secretary*. Can you believe that? I was almost angrier at him for being such a cliche than I was for the cheating."

"Well good riddance," I say.

When I stand up again, I collide with something. It's

Emma, who's taken a step too close to me in her slightly buzzed state. She stumbles—and then with a loud *crunch*, her elbow goes right through the drywall beside us.

Emma's eyes widen instantly as she rights herself. "Oh my—Nikki I'm so sorry, I broke your house. I'm such a lightweight. I'll pay for the repair, okay? I'm so sorry."

I wave her off, my eyes still focused on the hole.

"It's... fine."

Right now, I could care less about a little hole in the drywall. I'm much more concerned with the fact that I think there's another *room* behind it.

TWENTY-THREE
NIKKI

Emma stops apologizing as she realizes I'm still staring at the wall.

"What? I'm telling you, that'll patch up easy. Remember junior year, when I was trying to impress Bobby the Boxer? How…"

She trails off as I set down my glass on top of the wine cooler and then crouch beside the hole.

"What is it? Is there something back there?" she asks.

My throat is dry as I bring my face closer to the hole. I'd expect to see pink insulation or something behind the broken drywall, but instead there's just… darkness. As my face comes even with the hole, I feel the slightest pass of air.

What is this?

"There's definitely more space back there, but it's been covered up," I say slowly.

"*What*? Let me see," Emma says, setting her glass beside mine before crouching down.

I move aside so she can peer through the hole. While

the light from above doesn't reach very far into the hole, it's obvious there's more space back there.

"Weird..." Emma says. "I wonder what's back there."

"I do too," I say.

Emma glances over at me, a slightly devious look in her eye.

"After the week each of us has had... I don't know about you, but *I* could definitely break something."

After a moment of deliberation, I nod. I've got to know what's back there.

Also, it's my house, not some place I'm renting. That means I'm entitled to remodel however I see fit.

We stand up and make our way to Noah's workout bench. Underneath it, there's a row of dumbbells of differing weights.

Emma and I each grab hold of a seven-point-five-pound dumbbell and then walk back over to the hole in the wall.

She gives me another raised brow look, just to make sure it's okay. I let out a breath and then nod to her.

Grinning with anticipation, Emma grips tight to the base of her dumbbell and swings it around, letting out a little shriek as it slams into the drywall in a puff of white powder. She wrenches the weight out, with a smile on her face as she flicks her hair back.

"That felt good, Ki."

I tighten my grip around my own weight and step up to the plate. Batter up.

The dumbbell crashes through the drywall with a loud crack, this time breaking off a large piece that collapses inward.

Emma was right. That *does* feel good. We swing freely now, taking down the rest of the wall in less than five minutes.

When we're done, the two of us stand in what is now clearly a doorway, shoulders heaving and foreheads slick with sweat.

Emma lets the dumbbell drop to the floor at her feet, and we gaze into the darkness.

"I really needed that," she says, panting slightly as she pulls out her phone.

Turning on the flashlight, she shines it into the darkness to reveal... a big hole.

At least, I think that's what it is. There's more cement at our feet, but only for another six inches or so before it all becomes dirt. As Emma shines the flashlight around the walls, I see those are made up of dirt, too. The ceiling is low, low enough that Emma needs to hunch slightly to fit inside.

"What in the world?" Emma says, taking a step in.

She lets out a shriek that makes me scream too, only for her to break down into laughter a moment later at my reaction.

"Just a spiderweb, sorry," she says, shaking out her leg as she chuckles.

I shake my head but step inside with her, holding out my own phone flashlight now. It's most definitely a dug-out hole, with the back wall maybe ten feet away from where we now stand.

Why would somebody dig a room out of the dirt like this?

"Ki, come look," Emma says, drawing my attention.

She's standing close to the wall opposite me, her flashlight shining on something.

"What is it?" I ask, coming around her shoulder to get a look.

Her light illuminates a weird pattern of five lines that cut through the dirt, trailing downwards.

I look over at Emma who, while still holding up the phone flashlight, slowly places her hand up to the marks. That's when it hits me. These lines were created by *fingernails*.

Emma looks over at me, her eyes wide. I try to swallow, but it feels like my throat has closed up. Suddenly her head jerks up.

"Look—there's more."

She shines her phone up a foot higher on the wall, where another scratching pattern can be clearly seen. With the light raised up, I spot even more scratches in the corner. And on the ceiling. My heart beats faster and faster with every discovery.

"Emma..." I say, taking a staggering step backward as I shine the light fully on the dirt ceiling.

She looks up—and gasps.

The surface of the ceiling is *littered* with scratch marks. Everywhere I shine the light, there's more markings.

It's like the hole was hollowed out by hand.

TWENTY-FOUR
NIKKI

There are so many questions racing through my mind right now.

Why is this hole here?

Why was it boarded up?

And finally, and most importantly, why does it seem like it was created by hand?

The empty blackness and stifling silence of the earthy cave provides no answers. After quickly shining the light down the length of it—which reveals nothing more than the rough dirt of the end wall—we step out and back into the basement.

Emma shakes her head as she turns off her phone's flashlight. Her hair is pasted to her forehead with sweat.

"That is weird. *Really* weird."

I grab my glass of wine by the stem and chug it, letting out a breath only once I'm finished.

"Hello?"

Our heads snap up as my pulse skyrockets then drops

to a normal pace again. It's only Noah, having finally made it home from work.

"We're down here," I shout.

Emma steps over to me and reaches for her wine glass again. I hear the basement door open then Noah's thudding footsteps before he appears in front of us.

"You guys down here benching or something?" he jokes. "I didn't think—"

His eyes widen as he catches sight of the destruction behind him.

"What did you..." he starts but trails off when he gets a look at what's behind us.

"It's some sort of hole," I say to him as he makes his way across the room. "Like a little dirt room completely hidden by the drywall."

"Until I un-hiddened it," Emma says sheepishly into her glass before taking another sip.

Noah looks down at the pieces of the wall at our feet, carefully stepping over them before stopping in the doorway to the hole. He bends down and sticks his head inside.

"What's inside?"

I shake my head. "Nothing. You can see the other side if you go in there."

"The realtor definitely didn't mention this," Noah says after a few seconds.

She didn't mention a lot of things, as it turns out.

"Noah, there's claw marks all over the place. Like, fingernails. I think it might've been dug out by hand," I say, my chest tightening.

He pulls his head out to look at me. "What?"

Emma nods as I gesture into the abyss.

"All of the walls, the ceiling. See, look. There's some marks right there."

Noah nods as he looks around the cramped space. "And there's nothing else in here?"

"Nope," I say.

"This doesn't make any sense. Why was this covered up?" he asks over his shoulder with his body still facing the darkness.

After another couple seconds of looking, he pulls himself back out and straightens up. He claps his hands together to rub off the dirt.

"What do you think it could be?" I ask, clutching tight to my wine glass.

Noah gives me a bewildered shake of his head. "Old storage space, I guess? Still doesn't explain the marks, though."

Whatever it is, I don't like it. The musty scent of the hole seems to leech its way out, reaching my nose and making me take a step back.

"Let's go back upstairs. I don't want to be down here anymore," I say.

Emma nods and finishes off her glass of wine while quick-stepping to the staircase.

Noah grabs the second bottle of wine I pulled out and then follows us up the stairs. He switches off the basement light at the top and shuts the door behind him before letting out a breath.

"Just when I thought this week couldn't get any weirder," he says before shaking himself and pulling me into a hug.

"But anyway—hi," he says, kissing my forehead since we didn't greet each other when he came home.

"Emma, wonderful to see you as always," he says next, stepping away from me to hug her too.

"Thanks for having me. And sorry for blowing up your wall," she says.

Noah shakes his head. "No, that was a good find, you guys. Kinda freaky to think that was down there, and we had no idea."

I nod silently, my mind still trying to work through the discovery. I don't know what it means, but it can't be anything good.

We all make our way into the kitchen area as Noah opens the second bottle and pours each of us another glass.

My head lifts as I hear some kind of noise from outside. Like a party, or something. Noah hears it too, and our eyes meet for a moment before he sets down the bottle and races into the living room.

I'm right behind him, with Emma bringing up the rear, her glass raised so she doesn't spill.

I peer through the front window blinds with Noah as we watch a man and a woman walking down the street. They turn at Jenna and Mark's house, making their way up the driveway before moving out of view.

"Some work event," Noah says sarcastically.

As we watch, another couple comes from around the other side of the cul-de-sac to make their way toward the house. When Noah cracks the window, we can hear the distinctive noises of a party.

Seems like everyone but us was invited. I sit back

from the window as Noah presses it shut again and locks it.

"Well... we'll have our own party," Emma says, raising her glass.

And that's exactly what we do.

It's been a very long, hard week for me, and my best friend is here after not having seen her for a while. Time to make the most of it.

Noah stays with us for a bit but then graciously ducks out to watch the game upstairs by himself to give us some girl time.

We laugh, we cry, we drink too much wine. By the time one AM rolls around, I'm feeling pretty tipsy.

We've turned all the lights off save for a single lamp beside the TV.

"Come get it Petey," Emma giggles, dangling one of his toys in front of the tiny dog.

She's sitting on the carpet with her back to the sofa, legs crossed underneath her. I'm lying across the cushions watching Petey with a big grin on my face as he plays tug of war with Emma.

Right now, everything is good.

The rest of the neighborhood is getting together for a party we weren't invited to, but so what? I've got my friend, my husband. My adorable little dog.

Petey lets out a ferocious growl and puts all eight pounds of himself into a heave, and Emma lets out a sigh like he's managed to best her as she finally lets go of the toy. Petey trots a few feet away triumphantly before plopping down to continue chewing.

Emma leans her head back until it's resting on the seat cushion, her eyes staring up at the ceiling above.

"I've missed you," she says.

I nod. "I've missed you too. A lot."

"You're my best friend, you know that? And it really, really sucks not having my best friend living nearby," she continues.

Her voice is thick with the alcohol as she talks, but her words make me tear up a little bit.

Yep, I've definitely had too much to drink—we're officially at the *sob-and-tell-each-other-how-much-I-love-you* stage.

"It's just that—" Emma starts, but cuts herself off abruptly as noise from the backyard brings both our heads up.

Our eyes meet.

"What was that?" I ask, my heart pounding.

TWENTY-FIVE
NIKKI

Petey's dropped his toy and is looking toward the back of the house now, too.

I sit up on the couch, feeling things swim slightly as I try to get my bearings.

It sounded like branches moving against the window. I get my feet onto the floor, my hand digging into my pocket for my phone to text Noah.

Emma grabs the arm of the couch to pull herself upright, and the two of us start taking steps toward the back of the house. Footsteps on the stairs as Noah comes down, having gotten my text.

"What is it?" he whispers.

I shake my head. At this point, who knows?

Together, the three of us move into the tiled kitchen area, taking different positions. Noah's over by the sink, while Emma and I are closer to the back door. The window blinds along the back of the house in the living room are shut, so right now I can't see a thing outside.

I'm almost too scared to look. What if I part the living room blinds to find a face staring in from the other side?

My ears strain as I try to pick up any other noise from the backyard, but I don't hear anything. Petey tags along at my feet, head raising and lowering as he goes.

"Anything?" I ask Noah, who's peering out the window over the kitchen sink.

He cranes his neck as he scans the backyard side to side. "Not that I can see from over here."

He steps away from the window and joins us at the back doors, propping up one of the blinds with a finger to peer out.

After another moment, he shakes his head.

"Animal?" he asks.

I'm not so sure. Was one of *them* back here?

It's almost *more* terrifying that we don't see anything, because now I'm left to wonder.

And it's the wondering—the constant, cyclical thoughts of trying to process every possibility that are starting to drive me mad. The unknown is truly terrifying.

Noah remains watchful for another minute before finally stepping away.

"Whatever it was, it's gone," he says.

I don't know if it was one of our neighbors, or an animal. Maybe it was just some little fox on the prowl, rustling the shrubs in pursuit of a rabbit. I'd like to believe that. I run a trembling hand through my hair and look at Noah.

"I don't know how much longer I can keep playing this game," I say to him.

I'm exhausted, and not just physically. This suburban war we've got going on with Mary has utterly drained me mentally as well.

Not a moment goes by when I'm not consumed by thoughts and fears about what's going to happen next, and it's starting to break me.

Without realizing it was even coming, I start to cry. Mostly it's the alcohol, which tends to exaggerate my emotions, but still, this has all been so incredibly stressful. Just one thing after another, unrelenting.

Noah pulls me into a hug, with Emma coming up behind me and wrapping her arms around me, too. Petey wedges himself into the triangle and raises on his hind legs to put his front paws on my shins.

We stand like that for almost a minute before I compose myself.

"Okay, I'm over it. Thanks guys," I say, my words a little thick and accompanied by sniffles.

Emma nods. "I'm coming back next Friday, as soon as I can get out of work. No way I'm leaving you two alone with all these crazies."

I smile and laugh, my cheeks still wet. "Thanks Em."

We hug again, and then it's time for bed. I'm still slightly nervous about the noise in the backyard, but at a certain point, you've got to sleep. The wine has my eyelids feeling like they weigh twenty pounds each as I brush my teeth and wash my face.

Emma's all set up to sleep in the guest bedroom and gives me one last hug as I step out of the bathroom.

"You're my best friend. I love you," she says.

"I love you too," I reply, feeling like I might start crying all over again.

I crawl into bed beside Noah, who hasn't yet put on his mouth tape. He's waiting until he can kiss me goodnight. We kiss, and then he lies back on his pillow to stare up at the ceiling.

"This is not what I expected our life to be like when we moved out here," he says.

My eyes dart over to him. "You aren't mad at me, are you?"

"What? No, of course not," he says, wrapping his arm around me.

"If anything, I'm pissed at myself for not doing more research. I just... I think I allowed myself to get caught up in what a good deal we got on this place and didn't want to ruin it, you know?"

I nod silently as Noah holds me. He strokes my shoulder in silence for a while before speaking again.

"But we'll get through this. Together, okay? We'll get through this."

I scoot up and kiss him again before finally we say our *love yous* and *goodnights*.

MY HEAD POUNDS as my eyes crack open the next morning. The hangover is here in full force. As usual, the drum of lawn mower engines drones on from somewhere in the neighborhood.

Noah is still asleep beside me, his chest rising and

falling peacefully as he catches up on sleep from the week.

Sliding out from underneath the covers, I stifle a yawn and creep to the bathroom.

Once I'm finished in there, I tiptoe out of the bedroom to go check on Emma. Her door is cracked, so I poke my head in.

"Good morning," I say, my voice hoarse as I squint into the room.

"Not too much good about it," Emma groans.

I chuckle in agreement and rub my face. Together we head downstairs for breakfast and, more importantly, the lifesaving magic of coffee.

A quick glance out into the backyard shows that everything remains unchanged. Does Mary take the weekends off?

Not wanting to think much on our stroke of good luck, Emma and I spend the morning and early afternoon drinking coffee and chatting on the couch. Noah finally gets up around two PM and comes down the stairs.

"What's the report?" he asks.

I shake my head. "Doesn't look like anything."

Noah's eyebrows flick up. "Oh. Good."

Emma and I decide to take the car and get out of the house, because I'm definitely going a little stir crazy from having been cooped up all week between the weather and lack of transportation—not to mention my reluctance to spend any time outside in sight of my neighbors.

A little shopping trip is just what I needed, and by late afternoon, I'm feeling better.

It's strange, leaving the neighborhood and reentering

the real world. It's like passing into a different dimension, almost.

There's a moment I almost find myself wondering if I've imagined all the events of the past week, because everyone around us in the stores is so normal.

No watchful neighbors. No vengeful ones, either.

Noah stays home to cut the grass so we don't get another fine from Mary. I won't give her the satisfaction. Soon enough however, it gets near to the time Emma has to be heading home.

We load her bags back up into the car, and then I drive her to the station.

"I want you to call me every day, okay?" Emma says as she gets out of the car.

"I'm just as invested in all this as you now. And text me Friday-ish if you still want me to come up."

I pull her into a hug. "I'm sure I will."

Who knows what the coming week has in store for us? Even thinking about it makes my skin prickle a little.

Getting to see Emma at the end of the week is starting to feel like a reward for surviving another seven days in suburban nightmare land.

We hug for another couple seconds before finally she has to go. I want to beg her to stay but merely wave to her as she heads inside the train station. There goes my lifeline.

My footsteps are heavy as I round the car again and pull open the door. I want to drive anywhere but back to the neighborhood. I know exactly what's waiting for me there.

. Watchful eyes peering out from between curtains. Noises in the night. Footprints in the mulch.

The ever-present pressure that's already begun to build in my chest again as I think of the prospect of the week ahead.

Having Emma here was wonderful, but it's over now. Soon it'll be Monday, and that means Noah goes back to work, leaving me alone once again.

By the time I pull back into the neighborhood, the sun is no longer visible in the sky. It's still light out, given it's summer, but it's a dimmer light that seems to cast the houses in a strange filter as I drive down the street.

Someone is walking down the street, their back to me. I slow down, my heart racing. Who is that?

The woman turns her head of dark hair, and I see that it's Lily. Our eyes meet for a moment before she turns around hurriedly and starts walking at a faster pace.

I press down on the gas pedal and pull up alongside her, rolling down my window.

"Hey," I say, my heart beating a little faster.

Why is she trying to get away from me? Did something happen to her after the mask incident?

Lily glances over at me again and finally stops.

"What?" she asks.

Her tone is so harsh it makes me blink. She most definitely doesn't want to talk to me.

"I... you were right about the whole calling the police thing," I say, "I think they shattered our table in the backyard."

Lily's jaw flexes. "I *told* you."

She starts walking again.

"Wait," I say. "Please."

It's like she doesn't want to have to spend another second around me. Lily spins back around to face me, gritting her teeth for a moment before she speaks.

"Listen. They're messing with me again, okay? Because of *you*."

She shakes her head. "I *knew* I shouldn't have told you anything. I shouldn't even be talking to you now."

Her words sting.

"Lily, I'm sorry. I didn't realize any of this would blow back on you," I say, my chest tightening.

I don't want to lose Lily, too. She's the only person in this whole neighborhood who's been willing to talk to me, and now it seems like that's coming to an end.

Lily shakes her head. "I just... I just need you to stay away from me, okay? Please. It's the best thing for both of us."

I slump down in the seat as I watch her go. Great. The only other person in this neighborhood I knew I could talk to is now avoiding me like all the rest. As I pass her, I look into the rearview mirror.

There's a moment when Lily looks up, and our eyes meet. Then she looks away again, leaving me alone with my thoughts as I pull up to our house.

The lawn looks pristine, like all the rest.

I step out of the car and slam the door shut. Seems like one way or another, Mary gets what she wants. How can I beat a woman who has literally everyone under her thumb, whether by fear or something else?

We're the new kids on the block. Unable to upset the status quo. We're just expected to take it.

As I walk toward the house, my gaze catches on another yellow slip on the doorstep.

I'm really not sure how much more of this I can take.

TWENTY-SIX
NIKKI

The days of the next week pass in something of a haze.

I go to bed late, because I'm terrified of what *they* might do to the house in the night, only finally passing out when my body can't resist it any longer.

Thanks to the trouble falling asleep, I wake up late each day, and Noah's already gone, leaving me alone.

There's nothing to do, nowhere to go. No one to see.

More fines pile up. A new one each day. Chipped paint on the windows. Weeds in the driveway. Leaving the garage door open.

I'm drinking more than I ever have. Not just because I'm exhausted physically and mentally, but because there's really nothing else I can do. There's simply no way I can be creative in this state of mind.

No one comes to the door, leaving me to spend hours staring out the windows with a glass of wine clutched in my hand.

Watching has become my pastime. I've morphed into

that stereotypical nosy neighbor peeking through the blinds. The transformation is complete.

I see women walking in pairs while they jog. I drink. Couples going next door or across the street for dinner. I drink. Sometimes I hear laughter. I drink.

By Thursday, Noah mentions it. He looks at me with those kind eyes and tells me he's worried about me.

"It's just... you've been drinking a lot, you know? And it seems like you've hardly slept at all."

"Someone needs to pay attention," I say.

Noah sighs and rubs his face. "Listen. Why don't we go somewhere this weekend? Just get out of here, spend some time away. I think it could do us some good."

I chew my lip. "What if they do something to the house while we're gone?"

Noah throws up his hands. "And what if they don't? Are we really going to spend the rest of our lives like this, always peering through the windows? Wondering?"

"That's probably what They want," I say quietly.

Noah looks at me for a moment.

"I don't know what you want me to do," he says finally. "How do I help you?"

I shake my head. "I don't know."

He walks over to me and pulls me into a hug. "I'm worried about you," he says into my hair as we hold each other.

I feel my eyes grow wet. "I'm worried about me too."

This silent war with Mary seems to have pushed me to the breaking point.

Not at any point since we've been married, or ever

really before that, have Noah and I not seen eye-to-eye. Somehow on top of everything else, Mary's managed to mess with my marriage, too.

It feels good to have Noah hold me though, and for a moment everything is okay.

Then I remember that within a few short hours, he'll be gone again. I'll be completely alone once more.

"I just... I feel like I hardly even see you anymore," I say. "I'm so tired of being alone."

Noah chews his lip. "Okay, I'm taking tomorrow off. I'll be here the whole day with you, okay? How would that be?"

I nod, swamped with relief.

"Then maybe if you're feeling up to it, we could go somewhere for the weekend. Maybe a trip back into the city," he says.

I perk up at the suggestion. "I like the sound of that."

Some New York City chaos sounds like the perfect antidote to the stifling silence of the suburbs. Even just thinking of being back among all those tall buildings has me feeling excited.

There's an energy in the city that I've never felt anywhere else, and I never realized before how *comforting* it was.

I sorely miss it.

"Okay then. It's settled," Noah says with a smile.

Since he's not going in to work tomorrow, we're able to spend plenty of time making dinner together before curling up on the couch to watch a movie. We talk the night away, just enjoying each other's company.

It's a brief glimpse into what life could've been like every day, had we ended up moving somewhere else.

Once bedtime rolls around, Noah and I crawl into bed together. We cuddle some more, even once the lights are off.

Though I've been going to bed extremely late the past few nights and would normally be wide awake at this time, I'm able to drift off in Noah's arms.

We wake up the next morning to the sound of loud knocking. My eyes pop open as I sit upright in bed. Noah stirs beside me, cracking an eyelid. Petey lets out a yelp from downstairs at the noise.

Noah rips off his mouth tape. "Was that our house?"

Another round of knocking answers that question. Our eyes meet for a moment before we dash out of bed, my heart pounding.

I don't know who is out there, but a look at my phone for the time tells me it's only seven AM. After our late night and the wine I've had over the past week, I don't feel overly refreshed as I pull on a robe and make my way to the bedroom door.

More knocking. It sounds urgent.

Petey's downstairs, yipping with all his might to alert us that someone is outside.

Noah is right behind me, stuffing his feet into a pair of slippers as he yawns.

We descend the stairs in a hurry. I lean to the side over the bannister to try and get a look at who is out there, but all I can make out is a shadow through the foggy side-light window panels.

When we reach the bottom step, Petey bounds up to us, all frantic at the unexpected morning commotion.

Noah looks through the square of glass in the upper part of the door, his eyes widening.

"Who is it?" I whisper, my fists clenching.

"It's... it's *Mary*."

I stare at him for a moment, thinking I misheard him.

But no, he said Mary. Mary's at our door, and she knocks again with force.

What do we do? Noah mouths to me.

I'm sure she heard us coming down the stairs. After another moment of deliberation, I unlock the door and crack it open.

Mary looks at me through the crack, a smile on her face.

"Good morning," she says, sounding pleasant.

"...morning," I reply after a moment.

My thoughts are racing. What is she doing here? I haven't seen her since the night of the book club. She's made a point of not being seen when she leaves the fine notifications too, so why is she here now?

"Beautiful day, isn't it?" she says, gesturing up and behind her.

I don't respond. I need to know what she's doing here.

"The past week has been... unpleasant, wouldn't you say?" she asks. "I must admit it made me sad, you doing what you did. But I'm all for saying *let bygones be bygones*. You're a young couple, after all, with lots to learn."

"I think we've all had enough of the unpleasantness, yes?" she finishes.

I can hardly believe what I'm hearing. Is this some kind of trick? I stare at her for another moment before finally giving a slow nod.

Mary smiles again. "Good. I'm glad to hear it. I trust that from here on out, you two will be nothing but the most gracious of neighbors."

My lips part to say something, but I don't. I'm still completely taken aback by this turn of events.

Is Mary really calling it off?

She nods to me. "Have a nice weekend. I'm sure we'll run into each other at some point."

And with that, she's turned around and is walking back down the path toward our driveway. I watch her another moment before slowly shutting the door.

Then I turn to Noah, whose mouth is hanging open.

"Did that really just happen?" he asks.

I nod up and down. "I think... I think it might be over. Guess she figured we've had enough punishment."

Noah scoffs, runs his hand through his hair, and then smiles. "I'll tell you, I was not expecting that. Wasn't sure what I was expecting, but not that."

I have to agree. I have no idea what caused this change of heart in Mary, but I don't really want to question it.

Could this nightmare really be over?

For a moment, I dare to dream about a world where I can actually sleep soundly at night, knowing we're going to be left alone. We're never going to be friends with Mary, and probably not with anyone else around here, but that doesn't matter anymore.

At this point, I'll settle for apathy, which is leagues better than aggression. Live and let live is just fine by me.

Noah and I hug and then start making breakfast, excitedly talking between ourselves. Petey, little emotional barometer that he is, can detect the change of mood in the house, and he bounces around, happily flinging his roadkill toy with sheer joy.

It almost is like there's something different in the air. The sun is shining, and for the first time in what feels like days, I'm actually smiling and laughing.

We open all the windows to let in the glorious summer breeze, playing music on my bluetooth speaker as we dance our way through breakfast.

I let Emma know the good news, too. She responds immediately as always, saying she's glad to hear things have finally turned a corner. I also let her know there's no reason for her to come up tonight, because we're coming to NYC for the weekend.

Since Noah's off today, we have the whole day together. Nothing to do but have fun and enjoy our new home.

Now that I don't feel like I need to stay hidden away, we take the speaker to the back patio and enjoy the beautiful sunshine.

When lunch time rolls around, Noah fires up the grill

and we cook burgers. It's everything he's been dying to do since we've moved out here, and I can tell he's enjoying himself as he stands there with a spatula in hand.

I lounge on one of the chairs as Petey dashes around the grass under my watchful supervision. I've got a glass of seltzer on the arm of my chair. Droplets of perspiration glide down the length of the glass as I watch.

I've decided not to drink for at least a couple weeks, just to reset myself. Now that I won't be consumed by anxiety every waking second, it should be a lot easier to resist.

Once the patties are off the grill, Noah puts them onto buns and brings them over to me.

My first bite of the juicy burger leaves my mouth watering. Noah looks exceptionally pleased with himself at my reaction.

"Good?" he asks.

"Fantastic. My compliments to the chef," I say.

I end up having two, they're so yummy. For a guy who's never really had access to a grill, given he grew up in the city, Noah can really cook.

After lunch, we decide to take the party back inside.

We end up crashing on the couch, our stomachs full, cheeks and noses slightly sunburned. It's a scorcher out there today, and having spent the morning outside has left us with that slightly drained feeling that comes from hours in the summer sun.

Noah puts on a movie, but it's a lost cause. Within minutes, his head is dipping into his chest as he's lulled into an afternoon nap. It isn't long before I'm pulled under with him, drifting off as the warm breeze ruffles the curtains and cascades over me.

I'm gently awakened by Petey's growl as he wrestles with his toy. Opening my eyes, I lift my head up from Noah's chest to look around.

A glance toward the windows shows that it's nearly nighttime. The sky is painted with streaks of orange and purple, the sunset showing off its last-gasp colors.

I sit up a little higher as I work to pull myself out of the disorientation that comes with napping during the day. Reacting to my movement, Noah stirs.

Meanwhile, I'm turning my head from side to side, looking for Petey. I heard him, but I don't see him.

Finally, I spot him. He's not in the living room but on the tile behind us in the foyer. He's facing toward the front of the house, doing the head-raise-and-lower maneuver while he growls deep and low.

"Noah," I say, my heart beginning to beat a little faster.

Petey looks over at us for a moment before directing his attention forward again, the growl pouring out of his tiny body.

"Hm?" Noah says, still half-asleep.

I'm waking up quickly now and run a hand across my mouth to wipe away a line of drool.

"I think someone's outside," I say to Noah.

That gets his eyes open. He's got his head resting on the couch arm and turns it to look at Petey for a moment before looking back at me. Our eyes meet in the dim, dying light of the day.

Noah rolls off the couch and onto the floor before

crawling on all fours to the front windows. They're still open from earlier, and the curtains rustle again as a breeze comes through.

Noah brings his head up to peer between the blinds— and then immediately ducks down, sending my heartrate into orbit.

"What? Who's out there?" I hiss, instinctually dropping down to the carpeted floor.

My entire body tingles as I stare at my husband.

"They are," he hisses, his eyes wide as his mouth hangs open.

"Who?" I whisper, flapping my hands in anxiety.

Noah locks onto my face in the dim interior of the living room, his eyes wide with terror.

"*All of them.*"

TWENTY-EIGHT

NIKKI

I join my husband at the windows, my heart in my throat as I peer outside.

What I see drives my pulse to jackhammer level.

Standing in a half-circle in the street are what has to be at least thirty people. All of them are wearing masks like the one I found last week, and all are adorned in various articles of red clothing.

Flashlights and lanterns illuminate the spaces where their faces should be—only with the masks on, there are no faces to be seen. Just blank, sterile blobs of color that reveal nothing about the human underneath.

Inhuman. It's the most terrifying thing I have ever seen in my life.

Dozens of people standing there, faceless and nameless as they surround the house. Staring at us. Watching.

"What do we do?" Noah asks, his voice strained.

"Call the police," I hiss.

Noah nods quickly and pats his pockets for a moment. Then he looks over at the couch.

"I don't have my phone. Where's yours?"

I peer outside again, my mouth dry as I lick my lips. "I put it on the coffee table."

"It's not there," Noah says.

I whip my head around. "*What*?"

He nudges his chin. "Look."

He's right. There's no phone on the coffee table. Noah and I look at each other. This can't be happening.

"Where did you leave your phone?" I ask him.

Noah runs a hand through his hair. "In the kitchen I think, on the counter. Beside the speaker."

He races in a half-crouch across the carpet and into the kitchen but freezes there. My heart is beating so fast I can hardly breathe as he turns around to face me again, his eyes wide.

"It's not there."

That's when something moves behind him, drawing my attention through the open back door blinds.

"Noah," I say, my voice breaking.

They're in the backyard too.

Noah races over to one of the back windows, cursing as he looks outside before ducking down again. He's panting hard, his eyes glassy.

"They're everywhere," he says.

Another line of them, just standing there. Watching us.

Surrounding us.

Trapping us.

I can't breathe. My hands buzz as I look left and right, desperate for my phone. I know it was on the coffee table when I fell asleep earlier. I remember setting it there before I dozed off.

Now it's gone. What is going on?

Petey, sensing our panic, begins to whine in the foyer. Noah rushes back into the room as I wave Petey over to me, clutching the little dog tight as he jumps into my arms.

Noah pulls down one of the blinds again to look outside before cursing and whipping his head back and forth to look around the house again.

"No landline... what do we have for weapons?"

I hold Petey tightly, feeling his tiny body tremble against me as we stare outside.

The faceless watchers continue to stare back, unmoving. The sun has nearly completely set now, the last of the light leaving the sky like water down a drain.

My throat tightens. What are they waiting for?

They're almost as still as statues, only occasionally shifting the position of their lanterns or lights as they surround us.

Looking to the left, to the windows behind the tv, I see even more of them as they wrap around the house.

They've got us completely encircled within their faceless barricade.

"The car. We get in and just don't slow down," Noah says, snapping his fingers.

I nod and we push away from the window to the keyholder in the kitchen.

My heart nearly stops as I arrive in front of it. The keys are missing, too. My eyes move to the doggy door, and the box that's slightly ajar beside it.

This isn't happening.

I glance out the back door to the gathering of people in our yard. It's dark enough now that the glow of their lanterns illuminates the patio. One of them stands between the outdoor couches, in line with the rest as they form their circle.

Noah slams the counter with his fists. "What do they want from us?"

I have no answer. My eyes remain locked on the surreal scene in the backyard as I grab for one of the steak knives in the knife block on the countertop.

The blade is old and has never been sharpened, but it's all I've got. I don't know what they want from us, but I'm not going to go down easy.

I see blood, hear screams in my mind as I think of them shattering windows, forcing their way inside. Hands grabbing me, pulling at me. Pulling me apart.

Is that what this is? Some freaky ritual sacrifice situation?

My eyes flick up to the horizon, where I watch in real time as the last of the day's light leaves the sky. It almost seems to happen in slow motion, each second dragging itself out until there's nothing but night sky above and darkness below.

And then, as we watch, they begin to walk forward.

TWENTY-NINE

NIKKI

Noah grabs a knife of his own as we sprint back into the living room.

Our shoulders heave as we stand there, knives extended with our heads whipping back and forth to look through each window.

They continue to step forward, coming up onto the driveway, the lawn. Each step is slow, methodical. In sync. The net closes. The noose tightens.

Beside me, Noah breathes heavily, his sweat-soaked hand gripping tightly to his knife handle while his other arm wraps around me protectively.

They raise their lights higher and higher with each step. There's so much light and they're close enough now that I can clearly make out the red clothing worn by those outside.

That's when I notice that it appears to be... *stained* red.

That realization nearly has my knees giving out

beneath me as I let out a small whimper. Petey shakes like a leaf, and I squeeze him even tighter.

What happens next? Shattered windows, broken doors? Screaming and—

They've stopped. About ten feet from the house in all directions, they've stopped advancing. I blink, my pulse pounding so loud in my ears that I can hardly even think.

"Hey neighbors," a voice says from outside, as if it's just a normal Friday night.

I recognize it instantly. *Jenna.*

One of the figures moves forward, coming out from behind two others. Though she wears a mask, I recognize her build.

She's not wearing red, though. She's wearing white. Jenna makes her way to the front of the crowd and stops.

Noah and I remain frozen in the living room, half-crouched with our knives raised. I don't even want to breathe, in case that's the thing that sets everything off.

"Why don't you two come outside? It's a beautiful night," Jenna continues.

I peer through the open window, and Jenna's head turns, the creepy blank face mask snapping in my direction.

"There you are," she says.

"What do you want from us?" I shout, saliva flying from my mouth and landing on the windowscreen.

Sweat pours from my armpits down my sides as I stare out into the night. The glow from the lanterns makes the gathered figures look even more haunting than they already are.

Facemask Jenna tilts her head.

"Didn't Mary tell you earlier? We're ready for you to be a part of the neighborhood now," she says.

I blink hard, panting.

"We're ready for you to join us. Come outside," she says, waving us out with a hand.

"I'm not going out there," I shout back instantly.

Does she think we're stupid? Noah licks his lips beside me as we both look out in horror.

"But you and I are supposed to be sisters, Nikki. Join us—spill blood and make my robes red," she says.

My heart pounds. Is she serious? Is all this some kind of horrifying initiation into their cult or something?

"I'll never be your sister, Jenna," I shout through the window.

Jenna drops her head for a moment, as if my comment really wounds her.

"Hmm," she says. "I'm not sure that's the right answer, Nik."

Then I hear it. A strange sound coming from somewhere below us. A distant thumping, thudding.

The basement.

Noah and I look at each other and then pull away from the windows as Jenna speaks again.

"You'll join us, Nikki, you'll see. You have to."

Her words carry through the house as Noah wrenches open the basement door and flicks the light switch. The two of us race halfway down the steps.

The noise is even louder down here, and now I can tell where it's coming from—the dirt hole that was behind the drywall.

Noah grabs a flashlight off the step at his feet and

clicks it on, aiming it in that direction. The beam shines down the length of the hole and reveals a sight that has my stomach so tight I can't breathe.

Hands are tearing away at the back wall of dirt from the other side. Fingernails shine in the light as they grab clumps of dirt. Scraping, clawing.

"Oh my..." Noah starts, but his voice trails off in horror.

They're literally burrowing into the house. The hole in the wall was never a hole at all.

It was a tunnel.

For whatever reason it had been closed up before, but not anymore. Now, they're opening it back up.

"Trust me Nikki, you'll love it with us. Aren't you tired of living in fear of your neighbors?" Jenna says from somewhere above, her voice slightly muffled.

"We can make it all go away."

I lick my lips, unable to tear my eyes away from the clawing hands that continue to eat away at the wall of dirt. They're working quickly, tearing away chunks of dirt and widening the gap from the ceiling in real time.

My head snaps back toward the basement stairs as the front door handle jiggles. Then someone knocks. Loudly.

It's silent for two or three seconds, the time passing with Noah and I breathing heavily.

Then more knocking, this time on the windows. The siding. The back doors. All of them are knocking, creating a pulsing rhythm that continues to build in speed and intensity.

Noah's breathing so fast he looks like he might pass out, and I don't feel any better.

"Nikki..." he says, shaking his head.

I do a slow spin, trying to think of anything but the knocking, but it's impossible. Its constant noise seems to wipe away any other thought, my nervous system pumping adrenaline through a fire hose.

They're not just knocking anymore—they're pounding. Thud after thud as I blink hard, my mind spinning and heart racing.

The wall of dirt is nearly gone now too. Hands have broken through at the bottom, chewing away at the barrier from both sides. Within a minute, it'll collapse.

There's so much noise. Knocking, pounding, slamming. The very walls seem to shake with the pressure as dirt spills over. We're out of time.

I look back at Noah, who's got his hands on his head. We're completely surrounded. Within a minute, they'll be inside our home.

"There's nothing we can do," he says, his eyes tearing up.

He drops to his knees, his head still in his hands as the pounding continues. There's no way out of this. They know it, too. In a matter of time, they'll have us outside.

The pounding is unrelenting. It makes my teeth rattle as an idea strikes me. Desperate, stupid. Our only hope.

I grab Noah to get his attention and point.

Mary and the rest of them might think they know me, but they don't. They want us to come outside, to join them. To give in.

But see, I've never been one to do what I was told—at

least not until recently. I might have lost myself over the past couple of weeks, but I am *not* a follower.

Not before this neighborhood and not now. In spite of everything I've been through, I'm still *me*.

So as the last handfuls of dirt are removed and the wall comes crumbling down, Noah and I are sprinting full speed into the dark, armed with a dumbbell in each hand.

THIRTY

NIKKI

I let out a grunt as I collide with something in the dark.

There's a shout of surprise, and we tumble, a mess of arms and legs. There's light at the other end of the tunnel in front of me, maybe another fifteen feet away. Noah and I have crashed into whoever was behind the wall like a bowling ball striking pins.

There's shouting, confusion. I swing hard, the cast-iron dumbbell connecting with a heavy thud as I make contact.

Someone lets out a wail, and the hand that grips my shirt releases. I scramble up, but bump into someone else. Another swing, but with the tunnel being as tight as it is, I don't have full range of motion.

Hands grip me like vices. Then I hear Petey let out a ferocious growl, and someone screams. Suddenly, I'm free again and scrambling toward the light, screaming Noah's name.

"Nikki," Noah shouts back from somewhere to my left.

I whirl around but can't make him out in the mess of bodies.

Arms and legs are everywhere as they struggle back to their feet from our surprise assault. A hand wraps around my arm and yanks me forward.

Noah, tugging me toward the light. He's covered in dirt, with a streak of blood bisecting his face. Together we run.

Shouting and screams from behind us in the tunnel. The element of surprise is gone. We reach the other end, and I blink hard as the bright overhead light scalds me.

We're in a different basement, I realize with a jolt. There's dirt all over the floor at our feet, but besides that, it looks entirely normal. This has to be Clara and Bill's basement.

They've been digging a tunnel from their house to ours.

My mind flashes to the image of Bill standing outside on the patio, his shoulders rising and falling.

A break from the dig.

Footsteps in the tunnel, followed by more shouts. Time to run.

We bolt across the basement floor, pounding up the steps as fast as we can. Petey is a lightning bolt at our feet, a blast of white fur that shoots up to the top of the staircase in an instant.

The door swings wide as we burst out onto the first floor, chests heaving.

It looks like the quintessential American suburban home up here. Pristine couches that coordinate with the drapes. Family pictures on the wall and counter tops. Magnets on the fridge.

We don't stick around to admire the décor for long, because there's only so many more seconds before the watchers outside realize we're not in our own house anymore.

Noah, Petey, and I race through the home, shoving aside dining room chairs as we cut across the house. Theirs is laid out exactly like ours, and Noah yanks open the door to the garage a moment later. The garage door itself is closed, so we run to the door against the back wall and get that open before spilling out of it into the dark night.

There's shouting in the air, seemingly coming from everywhere. They know we've run, and they're coming after us.

I can hardly think as I follow Noah in the dark, my eyes trained on his back and my lungs burning. We're sprinting through backyards, branches and shrubs tearing at my face and knees as we run.

I push my legs hard, putting everything I have into the steps as we burst through a row of tall arborvitae trees into another backyard. This one has an inground pool, the water quietly bubbling away as we look left and right.

I'm soaked in sweat, and I think maybe some blood too. Where are we?

Shouts echo out in the night as They continue to hunt us down. Peering behind me, my heart rate once again skyrockets as I catch sight of a wobbly light through the tree line.

They aren't far behind.

"Come on," I say to Noah, grabbing hold of his forearm with my hand.

We run down the length of the side yard and into the front yard, our eyes scanning the street. We're a few houses up from the cul-de-sac. Looking down into it, I see dangling lanterns and swinging flashlights as They search for us.

I look up. That's Lily's house, to our right.

Licking my lips, I tug on Noah again and we sprint across the pavement. My muscles burn, screaming at me to slow down, but that's not an option.

Knowing we might be spotted at any second, I point, and Noah nods, both of us running into Lily's side yard.

There's a small wooden fence there that Noah vaults in one go, landing with a grunt on the other side. I come up against it, heart pounding nearly out of my chest as I grab hold of Petey at my feet and hand him over.

Then I'm climbing over it myself, Noah's sweat-soaked palms helping me.

The shouts are nearly on top of us now. We make it around the side of the house and into Lily's backyard. There's a garden table with a few chairs around it and a shed in the back of the yard. I run to her back door and pound on it, my chest heaving.

Noah is doubled over just behind me, gasping for breath as droplets of sweat drip off his hair to land on the patio stones.

Come on, where is she?

I knock again, my face twisting as I try to peer through the blinds.

"Lily, it's me—it's Nikki," I hiss.

More shouts from the street.

Finally I see motion behind the blinds, and then Lily cracks open the door. Her eyes widen as she gets a look at me on the back doorstep.

"What happened? What's going on?" she asks.

She's got her hair in a bun and is wearing a tank top.

"Let us in," I pant.

Lily steps aside, and Noah and I scramble inside instantly. She shuts and locks the door and then peers through the blinds before turning back around to face us.

The interior lights are off, and her curtains are shut as usual. For now, we should be okay.

"They came after us," I say, gasping for air. "It's happening. Right now."

Lily looks between the two of us as Noah nods, wincing as he clutches his side. Lily walks across the living room to the side window and peeks through the blinds, only to pull back a second later.

"The cul-de-sac is crawling with them," she says. "Looks like they haven't made it up here yet, but they will."

She turns to me. "Why did you bring them here?"

"Because you're the only one who can help us. Please, let's go. All of us—let's just go. You've got your car in the garage, right? Let's just get in and drive," I plead.

Lily chews her lip for a moment and then nods. "Okay. Okay. Let me get the keys."

She steps back into the kitchen, her head whipping back and forth for a moment before she scoops the keys up with a jingle.

"What do we do if they try and stop us? We don't have any weapons," Noah says.

Lily looks at him, her eyebrow cocking.

"What?" I ask.

She nods, chewing her lip. "Noah—go into the butler's pantry room and grab my gun while Nikki and I get the car started. Black case, first drawer. *Hurry*," she says.

We break apart, Noah dashing toward the back of the kitchen while Lily and I make our way to the door to the garage. She pulls it open, revealing the dark space.

Her car sits silently in front of us. Outside, the muffled shouts continue.

We each race around to opposite sides of the car and pull the doors open.

"Up Petey," I say, slapping my leg and dropping into the front passenger seat.

He leaps up into my lap as Lily gets into the driver's seat and shuts her door.

She hunches forward to insert the key into the ignition and then pauses.

There's a second of silence filled with our panting as I look over at her.

"What?" I ask.

"I might know a way to get them to stop," Lily says.

"What? How?" I ask, looking over at her.

Lily lowers her hand from the ignition and turns her head toward me.

"Join us," she says.

I blink, confused for only a moment before it hits me. Join—*Oh no.*

I start to tremble in the passenger seat, suddenly realizing how dark the garage really is. Lily's smiling now as she nods.

"We're interested in you, Nikki. We want you to join us. To become one of us."

I can't believe this is happening. Lily is one of *them*.

All this time, she's been one of them.

"The fear, the anxiety, it all can go away. Join and life becomes easy, even welcoming. There is more being scared," she says.

The shouting from outside seems to be drawing closer. Lily shifts in her seat, the leather squeaking slightly as she twists her body to face me.

The door to the house is still standing open, letting a small stream of light into the garage.

Noah.

"Where's Noah?" I ask in a trembling voice, my throat so tight I can hardly speak.

Lily shakes her head. "Don't worry about him. We're interested in *you*."

"What have you done?" I ask.

Lily opens her mouth to speak again, but something behind her draws my attention. Movement in the shadows—and then there's a crashing noise and glass everywhere as the driver's side window bursts into dust.

Lily lets out a scream and tries to turn around, but it's too late. A hand grips the back of her head and slams her face into the steering wheel in a flash, making me jump.

Lily's body crumples like a ragdoll in the seat. The door opens, and she tumbles out onto the garage floor.

I can't move. My body is pressed up against the other

side of the car, my chest rising and falling as I try to think, to imagine who could've just knocked Lily out cold and saved me.

Nothing can prepare me for seeing *Mary* settle into the driver's seat.

THIRTY-ONE
MARY

When Ron and I first moved to Peerskill, we were so excited.

I'd spent almost two decades in New York City and was finally ready for a change of pace. So when Ron got the confirmation that his job would be switching to mostly remote, we started searching for a house.

Our own place. Own our space, all to ourselves.

I can still remember the giddiness I felt on the first night we spent in our new home.

Excited and a little nervous for what lay ahead of us. That next morning though, there was a knock at the door.

If only I'd known then what I know now.

A woman who called herself Lily was on the doorstep, offering us a plate of homemade cookies she'd made, just for us. All smiles.

Ron and I were of course delighted. Being a little older than most of the other women I'd seen around the neighborhood, I was pleasantly surprised that an effort was being made to help me fit in.

Next thing we knew, it seemed the entire street was lined up outside, all of them offering their congratulations and baked goodies.

We were invited to backyard parties and barbeques. Dinners at neighbors' houses. Despite the gap in our ages, I really felt like Lily and I were growing close.

For a few days, everything was truly fantastic.

And then... it wasn't.

I remember the exact day things began to change. After everyone had been so hospitable, Ron and I wanted to return the favor, so we decided to invite a few folks over for a dinner party of our own.

In an abundance of caution, I'd asked every single person I'd invited about any possible food allergies I needed to be cognizant of when preparing a meal.

A few told me about nut allergies and shellfish, but that was all. I even wrote down exactly what I couldn't use, so it wouldn't slip in somehow by mistake.

I wanted to do everything right.

So when Lily, after taking a bite of cake, suddenly gasped and asked if it had egg in it, I was horrified.

Of course there was egg in it. I'd used egg because, well, that's how you make a cake. And I *knew* that when I'd asked her, she'd said she didn't have any food allergies.

But then there she was, tears running down her face as she ran to the sink to spit up the cake. The entire dinner party watched, their mouths hanging open, as Lily shouted at me for trying to kill her.

I could do nothing but apologize profusely. If I'd known she'd had the allergy, I'd never have made some- thing that contained eggs. Only Lily insisted she *did* tell me about it, and she couldn't believe how little respect I had for her and her wellbeing.

From that night forward, things were different.

All of a sudden it seemed like the folks who'd usually wave to me as I worked in the garden walked by a little faster, barely even acknowledging me. Then they started ignoring me altogether.

One day, there was a yellow slip on my doorstep.

A fine for parking in the driveway, as opposed to inside the garage.

I hadn't even thought to check the HOA rules, because Lily, the head of the association, had previously assured me things were very relaxed around here.

That wasn't the case anymore. I could count on one hand the number of days over those next two weeks we didn't receive a fine for one thing or another. It put a strain on Ron and me, and we began to fight more than we ever had before.

Luckily though, we always managed to resolve our disagreements. It was us against them, after all.

Things started to break around the yard, too. It seemed like something had chewed through the bottom of the back fence, meaning we had to replace it. Window screens would show holes the day after a windy night.

Ron seemed to think all these things were coincidental, but I did not. I knew Lily was behind it all, but I couldn't quite figure out why.

Yes, there had been the allergy incident, but I knew she hadn't told me about being deathly allergic. I may be older than her, but I'm not that old. I have the best memory of anyone I know.

To me, it was clear she'd omitted the information on purpose, almost like she'd *wanted* me to mess up.

But why?

That was what I couldn't wrap my head around. She'd ensured I would fail and then began to punish me for doing so.

Did she get some sadistic pleasure out of it?

After another week of the nightmare, we found out.

All the neighbors were outside the house, dressed in red with these masks on that completely obscured their faces.

They wanted us to join them. All the annoyances, fines, ostracization—it had all been some sort of twisted hazing ritual, meant to test us.

Apparently we'd passed, and that meant we were now welcome to join. Ron *insisted* we join. I think he was just desperate for it all to end.

So I joined.

At least, that's what Lily and the rest of them assumed.

Sure, I walked outside and was given a mask of my own. I let my hand be cut, and the blood from the wound soaked into one of the other member's sweatshirt, turning it from white to red.

We were a part of them now.

That's when I found out about the tunnels.

Ron and I had heard weird scratching sounds late at night, but had assumed it was mice or something.

Turns out they had been burrowing from our next-door neighbor's house to ours. I can still smell the heavy scent of the dirt as I helped pull away the last few chunks of dirt to connect our house with the rest of the loop.

An entire tunnel system, connecting the circle of houses in the cul-de-sac with the rest of the street. A network that allowed the group to move unseen between houses, and all of them connected to the large chamber beneath the forested circle of the cul-de-sac.

That was where the sacrifices took place.

You see, the cult believes that blood must be spilled. The clothes must stay red. A bonding ritual, meant to bring the group closer through shared secrets and trauma.

We were told this bond would be what kept us together in the end times while the rest of the world collapsed around us. Us against the rest.

To the rest of them, I was an eager participant. I chanted when I was supposed to, helped clean up after sacrifices—even though I could hardly do it without gagging.

My resolve was the only thing keeping me together. The resolution that I would bring this whole thing down. Somehow, some way.

Before my first sacrificial ceremony, I was approached and ordered to provide every password I had —to everything. Bank accounts, emails. All of it.

They owned me. Blackmail, to be used in the case of me ever trying to leave.

That would be how I'd bring them down.

As I worked my way up the ranks, always with a smile on my face, I gathered what information I could about The Neighborhood, as they loved to call themselves. Even took pictures during a ceremony with a hidden camera.

Soon enough, I was the new head of the HOA. The more they trusted me, the easier it was to find out more information.

Over the course of the next two years, I built up a blackmail file of my own on The Neighborhood. Enough to send everyone to prison for the rest of their lives.

I was preparing to go to the police, even though this nagging thought remained in the back of my mind that there was still a piece missing. Some part of the puzzle I didn't quite understand yet.

Regardless, I shook off the feeling, resolved to finally expose The Neighborhood.

And then, just days before I was planning to go to the police, I saw my daughter Nikki moving into the house down the street.

THIRTY-TWO

MARY

Everything changed when I saw her.

My child, born when her father and I had just graduated high school.

I was young and had big dreams about what I wanted to do with my life. I wasn't ready to be a mother. Looking back on it now, I could see clearly the signs of postpartum depression, not that I'm making excuses for my decision.

Leaving my beautiful, one-year old girl was hands-down the biggest regret of my entire life. But the damage was done.

Even after I came to my senses, her father didn't want me to come back. I don't blame him. I had done what no mother should ever, ever do.

It was something I had to live with for the rest of my life, and not a day went by that I didn't hate myself for leaving. His family was much better off financially than mine was—I had no money to sue for joint custody or visitation, and I didn't deserve it.

I didn't deserve to know my brilliant, beautiful daughter. I'd failed her as a mother.

Sometimes, I went back into the city just to watch her. It was as close as I allowed myself to get.

One of the times I went to see her, they must've followed me. I don't know why—maybe to test my loyalty. There were always so many tests, so much *tightening of the bonds* between us.

When Nikki and I first spoke at the block party, I was terrified she would recognize me. I'd been watching her for close to five years—before that I hadn't been able to find her.

I worried maybe she'd recognize me from one of my trips into the city when I'd be there in the crowd to listen to her play bass. I was usually about twenty years the senior of anyone else in the room, and probably the only one with tears in her eyes at some heavy metal song.

It had been almost thirty years since I'd run away. Coming face to face with her after all that time, I nearly broke down into tears all over again, my heart beating so hard I could hardly stand up straight.

But there was no recognition in her eyes. To her, I was just another woman.

That both relieved and crushed me.

Some tiny part of me had hoped that maybe, just maybe, my daughter still had some long-buried memory of her mother from all those decades ago. She'd recognize me, we'd hug, and then all would be forgiven.

Then I'd scream at her to run, run for her life.

But that didn't happen—of course it didn't. This isn't

a fairy tale. I messed my entire life up, and this is my punishment.

Any memory of me was buried too deep, long since forgotten. I was her mom only in my own memory.

So in the end, I was partly relieved that there was no recollection. Because I knew what was going to be expected of me.

I had to show The Neighborhood I was loyal.

If I didn't, if I told Nikki the truth, they would've sacrificed my daughter, I'm absolutely certain of it.

I would've lost her for the second time in my life.

So I proved to The Neighborhood how loyal I was. It was the only way to ensure my daughter's safety. I couldn't save her unless I tortured her by my own hand.

To keep her alive, I had to try and destroy her.

That doesn't mean I didn't still try to help when I could. Even though I knew it probably wouldn't work, I still had to try.

The day we were all required to show up with baked goods, I made two separate plates. One with brownies, and the other with a cupcake that said *RUN*. I was hoping against hope that somehow, some way, Nikki would understand. That she'd leave her brand new house and just get in the car and go, never look back.

But she didn't, and so I had to do what no mother should have to do.

The hazing she underwent was harsher than any other candidate I'd tested before. I made sure of that, wanting to do everything I could to make certain The Neighborhood suspected nothing.

I was ever the loyal follower, moreso to them than even my own blood.

But it broke my heart, seeing how much it affected her. I got updates every day from those in The Neighborhood who were assigned to watch the house.

Little by little, my beautiful daughter was coming apart. There were so many days when I thought about just rushing across the street and telling her to go, but I knew I couldn't.

They'd stop us before we made it to the garage. There were always people watching. Patrols, two-person teams that ensured accountability and adherence to the doctrine. No one even went jogging by themselves— everything was planned and monitored.

So I kept it up, while at the same time desperately trying to figure out a way to get Nikki out of here.

I wasn't going to fail my daughter again.

Her showing up here was the ultimate test. To see if I truly believed in the cause.

It also revealed to me the final piece of the puzzle, the part that had eluded me up until her arrival.

See, if I had gone to the police before with what I thought I knew, I would've had an incomplete picture.

It took my daughter showing up here for me to realize that.

Well, my daughter and my husband showing up with her, only he now introduced himself as *Noah*.

I look over at Nikki, who's still staring at me with wide eyes as she cowers against the other side of the car.

My daughter. My beautiful, brilliant daughter.

And she has no idea. Our eyes hold for another few seconds that feel like an eternity sitting there in the darkness of the garage. My heart pounds, and my throat tightens as I work up the courage to tell her the truth.

It's now or never.

"Nikki," I say. "I'm—"

The light in the garage flicks on, making both of us jump as we look toward the doorway to my right.

Ron—or Noah, as he's calling himself now—stands there in the doorway, his arms crossed over his chest as he shakes his head.

My heart thuds heavily as our eyes meet through the windshield.

"Noah, hurry—help me," Nikki hisses, waving him forward. She thinks I've climbed into the car to hurt her in some way.

Noah ignores her, still staring me down in the driver's seat. I'm pinned to the leather by his gaze. My not-so-loving husband.

"Mary, Mary, Mary," he says, shaking his head. "I'm disappointed. I thought you were a true believer."

"Noah, what are you waiting for?," Nikki says, her voice breaking with desperation.

She still doesn't understand.

Noah tilts his head to look at her, their eyes meeting for a few moments before Nikki starts to shake her head.

"No," she says, her voice hollow with horror. "No, no."

The sounds of thudding footsteps fill the air around us as the other members of The Neighborhood filter up from the basement. Their masked faces fill in the space behind Noah as he steps into the garage. I recognize the build of the man standing just behind Noah. It's Roger, who was assigned the role of my husband while Noah was with Nikki. I dislike him almost as much as my real husband.

"You've been chosen, Nikki," Noah says. "When the end comes, you get to be safe. I've decided that. It's a huge privilege, and you should be grateful for it."

Nikki stares at him, her face pale. She's clutching her little white dog to her chest, who's started growling protectively at all the masked people who have appeared.

"I even ensured you have a friend here, someone who likes what you like. Didn't you notice Lily always wearing t-shirts of those loud bands you enjoy?" Noah says.

Nikki sits back like she's been stung by a tranquil-izing dart.

She's realizing, as I did, just how cunning and manip-ulative her husband is. He was seeing my daughter without me even realizing it. In fact, I bet that gave him some sort of sick pleasure, thinking of the day he would finally reveal her to me.

I lick my lips. I'm certain The Neighborhood has the house surrounded. But we're in a car. The keys are in my hand.

Can I get it started and backed out in time? The garage door is still closed. With each passing second, more and more members are filing into the garage.

"Join us, Nikki. You'll have a privileged place among us, as one of my wives," Noah continues.

"One of?" Nikki asks, her face white.

Then she blinks. "The rings."

"I should've buried them deeper. Should've known that little rat-dog of yours would find them," Noah says, making Nikki squeeze her tiny dog even tighter.

I look up at that. Wait a minute—that's right. When Nikki arrived at the block party, someone told me she was talking about having found two rings in the backyard.

Two, not one. I knew one of them was mine from my time with Noah, but whose was the other?

Lily puts a bloodied hand on the windshield as she pulls herself back to her feet with a grunt. Noah glances over at her, his face contorting with rage.

Of course. The original. The most dedicated.

"What did you do, Mary?" Noah hisses.

Two more members step into the garage. We're

running out of time. Without breaking eye contact with Noah, I slowly raise my hand beneath the dashboard and insert the key into the ignition.

Nikki sees it happening and tenses up, squeezing her dog tighter. She doesn't know me or trust me, but she wants to get out of here as much as I do, so she doesn't say anything.

Lily pushes off the hood, her bloodied face pitiful as she stumbles toward Noah.

Noah cups Lily's cheek as she sobs in his arms before his eyes hone in on me again.

"What have you done?" he hisses.

I push the key all the way in, my entire body feeling electrified as my eyes dart around the garage.

"To her?" I mutter. "It's *nothing* compared to what I'm going to do to the rest of you freaks."

Then I turn the key, and the engine roars to life.

The headlights flick on, temporarily blinding Noah, Lily and the other Neighborhood members as they shout in surprise.

It's only a second, but it's all I need to throw the car into reverse and stomp down on the pedal.

The car shoots backward, and Nikki lets out a shriek as we slam into the hard plastic and metal of the garage door.

In a screaming burst of sparks, we tear through it— and then there's more shouting as the rear of the car collides with a member who'd been standing outside it. There's a bump when we back them over, followed by a sickening crunch that I just barely register over all the other chaos.

The engine squeals as we tear down the driveway, and then grass and dirt is flying through the air as I spin the wheel and back us onto the grass, driving in reverse across the front yard.

I whip my head over my shoulder to look through the back windshield to see where I'm going, my knuckles white around the steering wheel.

In front of us there's screaming, shouting. Bodies fill the driveway as the members recover from their shock and give chase. Out in the street, glowing lights are everywhere.

"Go, go, go," Nikki screams beside me, her dog howling.

I throw the car into drive and floor the pedal, the tires spinning for just a moment before they find purchase, and we take off down the street.

People dive out of the way, and then lanterns fill the road behind us as they run after us, the screaming and shouting unrelenting.

Nikki is panting beside me, twisted around in her seat to look back at the blood-red figures giving chase behind us. We're putting distance between us rapidly as we move up the street.

Coming to a stop sign, I blow right through it, the car skidding and nearly going up on two wheels as I turn the wheel to the right, heading for the neighborhood exit.

Red and blue lights flash up ahead.

A police car, pulling into the subdivision. I take my foot off the gas and stomp on the brake, so we don't slam right into it.

The car skids to a halt.

"Thank you, thank you," Nikki says, her fingers scrambling for the door handle.

"Nikki, wait—" I say, but she's already out of the car and racing toward the officer.

"Help us," she screams, pointing behind her.

I open my car door too, shouting at her to get back in. She doesn't hear me. My heart pounds in my chest as I run up to her.

"—the whole neighborhood has gone crazy, some kind of cult," Nikki is saying, her words interspersed with gulps of oxygen.

"We need…" she continues, though her words trail off as she notices something in the passenger seat of Officer Breckman's car.

It's his mask and red sweatshirt.

Breckman looks over at the mask and sweatshirt beside him before looking back at me.

Then he nods. "Have you met my wife, Denise? Great lady. Makes a wonderful lasagna."

No. *No*. This can't be happening. It's like every single person I've interacted with since I got here is in on it—except Mary, for some reason.

I stumble back from Breckman's squad car, and into Mary. All of this is too much. The cult outside the house and the fact that my husband seems to be the *leader*.

Breckman draws his gun and points it at us before opening his car door and stepping out.

He cocks his head at the distant shouts of the other cult members as they charge up the street toward us. Within a minute or two, they'll all be here. There's nowhere else to run.

"Sounds like you've caused quite the stir, Mary," Breckman says to her as she stands beside me.

He nudges his chin at her. "Why'd you do it? Who is Nikki to you?"

I look over at Mary, who's already looking at me with a strange expression on her face. She seems... pained. It's not a look I've seen from her before.

Breckman rubs his forehead. "Guess it doesn't really matter. Okay you two, turn around. Great news, Nikki. You're finally going to get to see what we're all about. That's not such good news for you, Mary."

I see lights at the end of the street. The mob of cult members has reached the stop sign and is coming right for us.

It's over. Breckman glances up at them and smiles.

Petey, who's been doing his low growl this whole time, suddenly launches himself at Breckman's leg like a white bullet.

Then everything happens at once.

Breckman kicks out a leg, missing Petey's head by mere inches. Mary stuffs something into my hand while cupping my face with her other.

"I love you," she says.

"Now run. *Run!*"

She shoves me forward and then throws herself at Breckman, who's momentarily distracted by Petey's assault.

My shoes dig into the pavement as a gunshot splits the air.

THIRTY-FIVE
NIKKI

I jerk as the gun goes off, but I don't stop running.

Looking over my shoulder, I see Breckman pushing himself unsteadily to his feet, Mary's slumped form lying on the pavement in front of him.

Then his head snaps up to look around for me.

"Get back here," he shouts, running his hand across his face to clear the blood spray.

I duck into the trees, searching desperately around at my feet for any sign of Petey. A white flash of fur—he's here, thank God. I'm not going anywhere without him.

I'm still clutching whatever Mary stuffed into my hand in a tight fist—it feels like a flash drive. I pump my arms and race further into the dark trees.

The roar of the mob has reached a fever pitch now as they arrive at Breckman's cruiser. Glancing back, I can see their lanterns and flashlights through the trees as I tear through the forest, my lungs gasping for air. I have no idea where I am, or where I'm going.

It's pitch black, and I just took off in a random direction as Mary shoved me.

Why did she sacrifice herself for me?

I don't have another second to think about it, because I need to use all my mental faculties toward getting out of here alive. Maybe if I—

My foot catches on a root, and I come crashing down. I land hard, my knees slamming into sharp rocks and roots. I gasp and blink back the white spots across my vision as I struggle to get my feet back up underneath me. Petey's right there beside me, letting out a whine of urgency.

Like me, he can hear our pursuers crashing through the forest behind us. They're just a handful of seconds away.

They're going to kill me.

My own husband, leader of the cult, is going to kill me. Sacrifice me for whatever insanity they've all bought into.

Dragging myself back up to my feet, my palm brushes against my knee and comes back slick. Bleeding. I don't stop, limping the first few steps until I'm running hard again, my knees crying out. I ignore the pain, pushing myself to my very limit.

It's either keep going or stop and die.

Slender branches reach out and smack me, thorny underbrush tearing at my skin as I go. I'm squinting, barely able to see through my slitted eyelids as I stumble forward, knowing exactly what will happen if I slow down.

Suddenly I burst through the tree line. More pavement—another part of the neighborhood.

Houses stand silent in the night, porch and driveway lights falsely proclaiming just how normal and serene everything is here.

Hearing screaming from behind me, I take off down the street, my shoes slapping against the pavement as I go. Petey is right beside me, keeping pace as we sprint down the road.

If I can just follow this, I'll end up back on a main road where I can flag someone down and signal for help.

I just need to—I come to a halt. The road dead-ends about thirty feet in front of me. Nothing but more dark forest beyond it.

No.

I spin around to change directions, but the first of the lights has broken through the trees.

They're here.

Dark forms morph out of the shadows as they slow to a walk, knowing they have me cornered. I take a few staggering steps backwards, and Petey starts barking ferociously again.

It's a valiant effort, but it's over. I'm exhausted. There's nowhere left to run.

This is where it ends for me. On a quiet suburban street, on a beautiful summer night. Surrounded by adorable little homes all lined up neat and tidy.

Where the suffocating suburban serenity will muffle my screams. I pick up Petey and hug him close. Faithful to the end, my little pup.

In the distance, at the top of the road behind the members, headlights appear.

The backlighting enhances the menacing silhouettes of the figures as they advance on Petey and me. It's probably Breckman—or another Neighborhood member who doesn't want to miss the party.

For all I know, it's the freaking realtor.

The car starts down the road toward us. The members of the cult hear it too and drag their attention from me as everyone turns to look at the car tearing down the street toward us. It's picking up speed by the second as it approaches.

I suck in a breath, my entire side feeling like it's one big stitch.

Who is this?

Then the sound of heavy metal music reaches my ears, pulsing loud and deep.

It's still too far away to see who's driving, but I don't need to anymore.

I know exactly who's behind the wheel.

That right there, amid the thrashing drums and screaming guitar, is my best friend in the entire world.

Speeding toward us, Emma lays on the horn.

At first, no one moves from their position in the road. When they see Emma has no plans to slow down however, there are shouts and yells as they dive out of the way.

Emma cuts through the mob like a knife, the car racing toward me at top speed before she starts to turn.

The car curves around me, the brakes squealing as she pulls to a stop just behind me.

The gathered mob stands there stupefied for a moment before the roar starts up again, and they all charge forward.

"Get in," Emma screams through her open window.

I run up to the car and pull open the driver's side back door, gripping Petey and throwing myself across the back seat before locking the door. Emma stomps down on the gas, the car squealing again as it gets moving.

"How did you know to come?" I shout as we tear up the asphalt.

People are everywhere outside the car. Someone throws a lantern, which cracks the windshield and makes both of us shriek. Emma swerves around two masked people, pulling into the center of the street and leaving the majority of the cult behind us.

"I texted you, and you didn't text me back after two minutes," Emma says after taking a gulp of air. "Best friends text back immediately, unless something is seriously wrong."

I nod, wiping blood and sweat from my face as I pull to an upright seated position, gripping onto Emma's seatback as she swerves.

"Something *is* seriously wrong."

"Told you," she says with a nod, "Suburban crazy."

Suddenly she slams on the brakes, nearly throwing me head-over-heels into the front seat.

I lean to the side and peer through the windshield to see Breckman's car and Lily's car parked across the street, blocking it. Breckman gets out of his car, while Noah slides out of the driver's seat of Lily's car.

Emma throws me an *is-this-for-real?* look. I nod and wipe my face again.

She scoffs.

"And I thought my man was evil," she says.

Our car idles as Noah walks to the center of the two cars and stands there, his arms crossed in front of him.

Behind us, the mob marches forward with their lanterns and flashlights raised high. Red and blue lights from Breckman's cruiser reflect across the windows of the houses around us as we face off from each other.

"What do we do?" Emma mutters from between stiff lips.

She's gripping the steering wheel with both hands, knuckles practically white. I look out at my husband again, who casually leans back against one of the cars. He's got this smirk on his face.

He knows me. I won't run him over.

I love him too much.

All this he communicates as we look out across the space between our cars, our eyes having a conversation in the night.

"Nikki," Emma warns, her anxious eyes flickering up to the rearview mirror.

I chew my lip, glancing down at my ring finger. My husband has betrayed me in almost every single way imaginable. He knows me, yes—but really only a version of me.

The version I wanted him to see.

I'm a little ashamed to admit it, but I changed myself for him.

After Noah, I played bass less often and started watching golf more. I went to fewer live shows and wore more heeled shoes. Altering who I really was to please him, to make sure he was happy.

I'm thinking it's time for the old Nikki—the *real* Nikki—to be back.

"Drive," I say under my breath.

Emma glances over at me, her eyes wide. Then she presses down on the gas pedal. We roll forward, and Noah doesn't move.

He still thinks I'm bluffing, that stupid smirk hanging

off his face. The distance between our car and his body begins to close.

Thirty feet. Twenty.

Noah is still there between the cars, arms crossed. Our eyes meet again. Ten feet.

Now, he realizes his mistake.

"Married the wrong girl, sweetheart," I say, bringing up one hand to make a finger gun.

The other grips the car door as I brace for impact.

Noah throws himself back onto the hood of Lily's car just moments before we slam into the vehicular blockade. The two cars fly apart, bits of glass and metal arcing through the air amid a flurry of sparks as Emma and I scream.

We're through.

The engine roars, and tires squeal as Emma stomps on the gas pedal again. I turn around to look through the back window, where the street is littered with twisted chunks of metal from the collision.

Everyone is shouting, but I'm looking for my husband.

Noah is lying on the ground, chest to the asphalt in front of the police car. Looks like he avoided major damage. He gets an arm underneath him as bits of glass fall down from his hair.

Then I see Breckman, who's already shutting the door to his squad car, his determined gaze locked on us over the steering wheel. He hasn't given up the chase yet.

Before I can really process what's happening, my hand shoots up to cover my mouth.

I can practically hear the thud as Noah gets run over.

Breckman stops immediately, getting out of his car and looking underneath before his hands go to his head. He stares for only another second before simply turning around and running full tilt into the woods.

We're at the end of the street now, and Emma cuts the wheel hard. Before the scene is lost behind the houses, I watch as the rest of the group realizes what's happened. Some of them start running away, too.

Their leader is gone. It's over.

I turn around, letting my head rest on the back of the seat as I take a gulp of oxygen.

"What happened?" Emma asks over her shoulder as we tear down the silent street.

Empty house after empty house surrounds us. Shells. Disguises.

I open my eyes again.

"It's over," I say.

Petey crawls up into my lap, shaking hard. No doubt the car collision spooked him badly. I bring him up to my face and kiss him all over. If he weren't such a brave little dog, I think I'd be dead right about now.

I'm absolutely exhausted as we pull through the streets, navigating our way back to the entrance to the subdivision. We haven't seen another soul.

I ask Emma to slow the car down as we come up to Mary's body on the pavement.

"Are you sure?" she asks.

I nod and open my door. My footsteps seem loud in the quiet night as I walk toward her. When I get there, I find she's already gone. I kneel beside her.

I love you, she said to me.

The way she cupped my face made something stir in my chest, but there wasn't any time in the moment to try and figure out why. Now, sitting here beside her, I think I know.

A tear rolls down my cheek as I look down at her.

She sacrificed herself for me. So that I could live.

I open up my fist, revealing the flash drive she gave me. There's blood around the edges of it from where it cut into my palm, but I wasn't going to let it go for anything. I have a feeling that I know exactly what I'll find on this.

A shaking breath rocks me as the tears really begin to flow. Emma steps out of the car and comes over to me, holding me while I cry.

In my tears is a mixture. Relief, anger, loss. A letting go. Of everything I thought my life was made of.

When it's time, we get back into the car and start the drive back to the city.

EPILOGUE

NIKKI

TWO MONTHS LATER

I close the freezer door, my ice cream spoon hanging out of my mouth.

Today's flavor is birthday cake, one of my favorites. I get the lid open as I hear footsteps coming down the stairs behind me.

Emma appears, giving me a big smile.

"Date time?" I ask.

She's going out on a first date tonight with the handsome psychiatrist who lives on this block.

Emma nods and winks. "Time for my checkup with Dr. DeLuca."

"Good luck," I say to her, chuckling as I shake my head.

It's been an eventful few months, to say the least. When we got back to the city, we opened up Mary's flash drive. It had everything we needed to finally expose The Neighborhood cult for what it was.

Given the overwhelming amount of evidence, things moved pretty quickly after that.

Lily was taken into custody in the days following, as were most of the rest of the members. A few of them that fled that night are still on the run, though. Jenna is one of them. Officer Breckman too.

Interestingly enough, ownership of every single home in the neighborhood had been transferred to Noah's name at some point. Which meant that in the event of his death, all of the properties shifted to *me*.

I sold the lot of them to a developer, wanting nothing more to do with any of it.

Using the proceeds, I bought my dream townhouse on the Upper West Side.

It's a gorgeous three-story space with open, airy rooms, high ceilings, and a lovely private backyard where Petey can run his little heart out.

I asked Emma to move in with me. After she and Max broke up, we decided it was about time we went back to the way things should be.

Roommates, just like in college.

There was something else on Mary's flash-drive, too. A last-minute addition.

A long document where Mary shared everything she never got to tell me in person. I cry every time I read it.

I'm still trying to work through this mess of resentment and loss I feel about her. Writing songs helps a little. I thought I was past all this, but it turns out this kind of thing doesn't really just go away.

It's going to take me some time to figure out my feelings about everything, and that's okay.

So while Emma is happily dating again, I don't think I will be for a while. Not until I straighten myself out first. Lots of old, unresolved feelings to work through. It's going to be me and my bass for a while, and that's okay.

I've also realized that I was too willing to change myself for someone else, and I see that now. I tried to fit the mold of what I thought Noah wanted, and he took advantage of that.

So for the foreseeable future, I'm just going to focus on me and try to find joy in the simple pleasures of life.

Right now, birthday cake ice cream is at the top of that list.

I scoop some out of the mini cup and let the cold, creamy sensation melt on the heat of my tongue, shutting my eyes as the sweet flavors wash over me.

I've got the windows open, and the sounds of the city drift into the house around me. Horns, beeps, random banging.

I can't get enough of it. I'm a city girl, through and through. This was always where I was meant to be. I dig out another spoonful of ice cream, but before I can get it up to my mouth, the doorbell rings.

Maybe Emma forgot something. I set down the ice cream and hop off the couch as Petey trots up next to me. Always my little protector and travel buddy.

I cross the length of the house and go to the foyer to pull open the heavy door.

It isn't Emma on the doorstep, though. It's an older couple, a man and a woman. They've got a little cake on a plate between them that says *WELCOME!* in frosting.

Both of them smile as the door swings open.

"Hi there, neigh—"

The slamming of the door cuts them off.

Not this time.

THANK you so much for reading *Such Lovely Neighbors*. I hope you enjoyed it. If you'd like to read my FREE psychological thriller novella, The Weekend Trip, sign up for my newsletter at jackdanebooks.com. As a member of my mailing list, you'll be the first to know whenever I have a new book release and get behind the scenes information on my stories and my writing life.

If you had a great reading experience with this novel, would you mind taking a minute to post a review on Amazon? A few words is all it takes, and it will truly make a difference in my career as an author.

Reviews are so important in helping other readers find great books that are worth their valuable time and attention.

Thanks so much for reading :)

Jack

ALSO BY JACK DANE

THE APARTMENT ACROSS THE HALL

HIS FIRST WIFE

THE OTHER COUPLE

THE NEW SITTER

ABOUT THE AUTHOR

Jack Dane writes thrillers and psychological fiction that largely takes place in New York City, where he lives. When not writing, Jack enjoys going to jazz clubs, taking people-watching walks in the Park, and exploring the city by night, where he picks up ideas for his next book.

Get a FREE copy of his thriller novella *The Weekend Trip* by heading to jackdanebooks.com

You can connect with Jack on Facebook as well!

Printed in Dunstable, United Kingdom